Pickle in the Middle

PiCKLe iN the Middle

NORA M. BRAUN

AN AVON  CAMELOT BOOK

PICKLE IN THE MIDDLE is an original publication of Avon Books. This work has never before appeared in book form.

AVON BOOKS
A division of
The Hearst Corporation
1350 Avenue of the Americas
New York, New York 10019

Copyright © 1997 by Nora M. Braun
Published by arrangement with the author
Library of Congress Catalog Card Number: 96-96988
ISBN: 0-380-78635-4
RL: 4.9

First Avon Camelot Printing: March 1997

CAMELOT TRADEMARK REG. U.S. PAT. OFF. AND IN OTHER COUNTRIES, MARCA REGISTRADA, HECHO EN U.S.A.

Printed in the U.S.A.

OPM   10   9   8   7   6   5   4   3   2   1

For my parents and the brood of eight children they raised, without whom I never would have known the wonderful ups and downs of a large family.

And also for my husband, Art, and our daughters, Alison and Sarah, whose faith in me is my foundation.

Pickle in the Middle

CHAPTER 1

"You little snoop!" Lydia Barnsworth grabbed the cloth-covered book from her seven-year-old sister's hand. "Stay out of my stuff!"

Katie's blue eyes widened. "You left it out," she said. "I can't help if it fell open."

"Yeah, I'm sure it just jumped into your hands." Lydia glared down at Katie. "This is my private journal. Not for your eyes," she added.

Katie shrugged her shoulders and started rearranging the trolls on her shelf. "It was boring, anyway."

"You—you . . . you brat," Lydia stammered. "I should never have taught you to read."

"It wasn't you." Katie smiled smugly. "I'm just a born genius."

"A genius brat," Lydia muttered. She turned on one heel and hurried out the door. This was the last straw. Katie had already dumped the contents of her schoolbag all over the floor, torn the cover on the latest issue of

1

TeenTalk, and interrupted Lydia's concentration a zillion times. And they had only been home from school an hour!

"Mom," Lydia said as she burst into her parents' bedroom, where her mother was sewing. "I *have* to have my own room. Katie is such a pain."

Her mother looked up from the dress she was hemming and sighed. "I do wish you two would learn to get along."

"But she was reading my journal!" Lydia protested.

Mom shook her head. "I'll talk to her about respecting your privacy," she said. "Meanwhile, try being patient with Katie. You know she just wants to be like you."

Lydia wanted to scream. She didn't care if Katie looked up to her or to the man in the moon. All she wanted was a room of her own, a room where little sisters wouldn't be allowed. But she knew what her mother would say. She'd heard it before. They couldn't afford a bigger house, and her older sister, Sharon, would be going to college in another year. Then Lydia could have Sharon's room all to herself. But a year felt like a life sentence when it came to sharing a room with Katie!

"What do you think of your new dress?" Mom asked. She held up the red flowered dress she'd been hemming.

"It's not new," Lydia muttered. "Why can't I have a new dress for the carnival instead of Sharon's old one?"

Lydia didn't usually complain about wearing her older sister's clothes. Her mother kept only the nicest ones, and she knew how to make them look like new. But Lydia was tired of being the odd one out. Sharon had all new outfits because she was the oldest, while Katie got some new things to replace clothes too worn out to wear after Lydia had used them. It wasn't fair. Sharon and Katie got everything, while she was the pickle stuck in the middle.

"We can't buy a new dress for every school event," Mom said calmly. "You can wear the one we bought for your birthday if you don't like this one."

Lydia couldn't wear her birthday dress. Not again. Everyone in her sixth-grade class had seen it at least a dozen times. If she wore the dress a thirteenth time, bad luck and disaster were sure to strike!

"I'll wear the red dress," Lydia said grumpily. "But I won't like it."

She slipped out of the room before she earned herself a lecture. At least with Sharon being six years older than she, none of her friends had ever seen the dress before. Not that it really mattered. Mom did a nice job, but Sharon's dresses still looked like sacks on eleven-year-old Lydia. She needed more padding in the right places.

3

Lydia wandered toward the kitchen, looking for a snack. What could she eat that would give her hips by Friday? Or maybe a little bit of chest? She sighed to herself. With her luck, whatever she ate would give her fat feet instead!

Her fourteen-year-old brother, Mike, was already in the kitchen, making a sandwich, and the counter was littered with an odd assortment of food. Lydia peered at the concoction in front of Mike.

"Yuk! What have you put on your peanut butter?" she asked.

Mike looked up and grinned. "Well, Mom bought the smooth peanut butter, so I sliced up a cucumber," he said. "After all, you can't have P.B. without the crunch." He tossed a couple of extra cucumber slices into his mouth and crunched for emphasis. "Then, of course, you need ham and cheese for protein and a dab of mayo to blend the tastes together."

Lydia's stomach churned dangerously. Maybe she wasn't hungry after all. She looked at the ripe banana on the counter. "And I guess the banana is for dessert," she said.

"Why have dessert later when you can have it with the main course?" Mike said. He grinned at Lydia's gasp when he sliced the banana onto the sandwich. "It's a culinary work of art, worthy of great chefs."

"That's disgusting," Lydia said. Suddenly she didn't

4

care if she ever had hips. In fact, she might never eat again!

"If you're nice to me I might let you have a bite of my creation," Mike offered.

"I think I'll go call Jenna," she muttered.

"Wait!" Mike yelled as she bolted from the room. "Don't you want half my sandwich? They might even name it after me when I'm a great chef. And you could claim the honor of tasting the original creation!"

Lydia ignored his teasing. Her family was a royal pain. First Katie and then Mike. All she needed now was for five-year-old Erik to show up with one of his jokes. His sense of humor was definitely unique, guaranteed to drive her crazy. She headed for the family room, hoping she'd be safe there, and dialed Jenna Taylor's number.

As soon as the ringing was replaced by the familiar voice of her best friend, Lydia said, "Save me, Jenna. I have to get out of here."

She heard Jenna's laughter echo across the phone. "No problem, Lydia. Come on over. I'm listening to the latest Amy Hart CD. You'll love it."

Lydia sighed. Jenna was an only child who didn't understand what it was like to be in the middle of a pack of five. But she always listened patiently to Lydia's complaints about her siblings and offered an escape when things got unbearable.

"You're a lifesaver, Jenna," Lydia said quickly. "I'll be there in a few minutes."

She hung up the phone and hurried through the house. "Mom," she yelled, "I'm going over to Jenna's. Be home for supper."

A muffled voice came from the direction of her parents' room. It sounded close enough to "okay" for Lydia. She got as far as the middle of the driveway before the sight of her brother Erik made her stop in her tracks.

"What are you doing with my bike?" Lydia yelled. Dangling from Erik's hand like a limp snake was the chain to her bike. Circular pieces of metal resembling clock parts littered the ground.

"I'm fixin' it," Erik told her proudly. Lydia just glared. He looked at the chain, then back at his sister. "It was too tight."

"It's supposed to be that way," Lydia told him through gritted teeth. "How else can it turn the wheels?"

"Oh," Erik murmured. He reached down and picked up one of the metal circles from the ground. "Guess it needs these too?"

Lydia wanted to scream. She closed her eyes and made herself count to five. It was her worst nightmare. Her ten-speed in the hands of Erik the Destructo!

"Don't worry, Lyd. I can fix it," Erik said. He looked

at her with his pale blue eyes, round and innocent. He was great at taking things apart. If he could just figure out how to put them together again . . .

Lydia looked down at the mutilated chain. She might as well walk to Jenna's. It was only three blocks away.

"Go get Mike to help you," Lydia instructed. She shook her finger at Erik and added sternly, "I want my bike fixed by the time I come home, or you'll be in big trouble."

She hurried down the drive. If she jogged to Jenna's she'd have an hour before supper. Lydia sighed again. An hour away from the craziness at her house was worth working up a little sweat for.

CHAPTER 2

Lydia was panting by the time she arrived at Jenna's. Her friend swung the door open and stared at her.

"What took you so long? You look terrible," Jenna said.

Lydia groaned and moved past Jenna, leading the way to Jenna's room as if it were her own. She collapsed on the bed and closed her eyes for a minute. When her heart stopped pounding in her ears, she sat up.

"Erik decided to fix my bike," Lydia said. "And you know how he fixes things." She rolled her eyes toward the ceiling and Jenna giggled.

"Like how he fixed your watch, and your parents had to buy you a new one?" Jenna asked.

Lydia grimaced. "Not quite that bad. This time I think even Mike can put it back together. That is," she added, "if he doesn't die first from the strange sandwiches he eats."

Jenna flopped down on the bed beside Lydia. "You really do have an interesting family."

Lydia glanced sideways to see if Jenna was serious. She was. "You want them, you can have them," Lydia said.

Jenna rolled onto her side and propped her head up with her arm. "Really, Lydia," Jenna insisted. "Isn't it nice to have someone to talk to? It's never boring at your house."

"Yeah, it's a constant zoo," Lydia agreed. "Mike is either eating something weird or trying an even stranger science experiment. Erik runs nonstop, including when he's demolishing something to see how it works. Katie makes up imaginary people or snoops into my stuff. And when Sharon's ever home, she's talking on the phone or practicing her cheers." She paused to catch her breath. "Boring it's not."

Lydia took a deep breath and pushed it out through her lips. "What I'd like is peace and quiet like your house. And a room of my own," she added.

"It can't be that bad," Jenna said. "I think it would be exciting to be part of a big family. There's always something going on and someone to talk to. . . ."

It didn't matter how Lydia explained it. Jenna wouldn't understand. After all, Jenna didn't have to worry about hand-me-downs or sharing her room or being teased to death. But what Lydia wanted was to be like Jenna—an only child.

"Let's not talk about my brothers and sisters," Lydia

said. "What are you wearing to the school carnival on Friday?"

Clothes was one of their favorite subjects. And Jenna was the expert.

"I haven't decided yet," Jenna said. "Let's go through my closet and pick something out."

Lydia eyed the walk-in closet overflowing with clothes. "We haven't got that much time," she said with a grin. "I only have an hour till supper."

Jenna laughed and started rummaging through the closet. It took awhile, but finally the choice for the carnival was narrowed to two outfits.

"Wear the blue one," Lydia said. "It looks great with your blond hair."

Jenna slipped on the blue dress and swirled in front of the full-length mirror. "It does look nice," she said, then, "Maybe we'll see Tom there."

Lydia giggled. Jenna had the biggest crush on Tom Bennett. She was always hoping to see him. "What will you do if we see him?" Lydia asked.

"I don't know. Say hi?" Jenna looked at Lydia, and they both broke into laughter.

"He won't know what to say either," Lydia said between giggles. "He'll just turn beet red like he always does."

"He does not," Jenna said defensively. Then she smiled. "Well, maybe a little."

10

Lydia pulled herself up off the bed. "I'd better get going," she said. "I told Mom I'd be home for supper. And it always seems to be my turn to set the table."

It took longer to get home than it had to get to Jenna's. Lydia didn't think it was worth jogging. Maybe if she was late, someone else would set the table.

Her family was just sitting down for supper when Lydia came in the back door. Her mother paused as she pulled a gallon of milk from the refrigerator.

"Wash your hands, dear," Mom said. "We're ready to eat."

Lydia stopped by the table to give her father a quick hug. Her sister Sharon glared over at her. "You have to clean up after supper," Sharon said sternly. "I had to set the table and it was your turn."

Lydia made a face at Sharon before disappearing into the hall. Sharon always forgot the times Lydia did her work. Maybe next time Lydia wouldn't be so nice about it.

She took her seat at the table, the family said grace together, and then the chaos began. Bowls and platters passed in every direction. Lydia had to grab fast to fill her plate. Once Mike got hold of something it was sure to disappear.

"Did you have a good time at Jenna's?" Mom asked.

Lydia swallowed a bite of chicken. "We went through her clothes to pick out an outfit for the carnival on

Friday," she answered. "Jenna has a ton of clothes to pick from."

She watched to see if the comment had any effect, but her mother just murmured, "That's nice."

Katie snickered. "Yeah, I bet Jenna wants to impress Tom Bennett at the carnival."

"See, Mom," Lydia said, glaring at Katie. "She *was* reading my journal."

"No, I heard you talking on the phone about him," Katie protested. As Lydia stared in outrage, Katie's cheeks turned pink and she suddenly pretended a great interest in the food on her plate.

"Katie!" Mom exclaimed. "Haven't we talked about respecting your sister's privacy? That includes not listening in on her phone conversations."

"Yes, Mom," Katie said sullenly.

Lydia turned her head away to hide her smile. She glanced down at Mike's plate. "Gross," Lydia exclaimed. "Mike put ketchup on his mashed potatoes."

"So what," Mike demanded. "I like them that way."

"Me too," Erik chimed in. "Pass the ketchup."

"You two are gross," Lydia said.

Katie made a retching noise. "It looks like roadkill."

"Ick! You're making me sick, Katie," Sharon groaned.

"That's enough," Lydia's father demanded, his stern expression quieting any more comments. "Keep your eyes on your own plate if someone else's meal bothers you. And let's have some pleasant dinner conversation for a change.''

Just then Erik set his glass of milk too close to his plate, tipping the glass over. A white river splashed onto the platter of barbecue chicken, turning the liquid pink. Everyone froze as the pink river coursed along the table, dousing the bread and dripping through the cracks in the table leaf. It ended in a waterfall off the edge of the table, cascading right into Lydia's lap.

So much for a quiet family dinner, Lydia thought sourly as her mother dashed into the kitchen for paper towels. Jake, the family's golden retriever, darted under the table to help clean up.

Lydia was sure things like this never happened at the Taylors' house. Jenna was so lucky.

Maybe the Taylors would consider adopting another eleven-year-old girl?

CHAPTER 3

Friday morning Lydia woke full of energy. Today was the carnival! She dressed in record time and went down to breakfast.

"Good morning, dear," her mother said. "Fix yourself a bowl of cereal. Everyone except you and Katie have eaten."

Lydia grabbed the box of her favorite cereal and poured it into a bowl. Katie sat across the table, licking jelly from her fingers.

"Katie, you've got jelly in your hair," Lydia said. She frowned and shook her head. It was amazing that someone who was supposed to be so smart could be such a mess.

"Oh, Katie," Mom exclaimed in dismay. "You've got it on your clean shirt too."

Katie glanced down at her shirt and shrugged. "It dripped," she said, as if that made it okay.

"Well, go up and change before the bus comes," Mom told her.

Lydia watched Katie leave the kitchen. Then she looked at her mother. "Are you sure Katie's a genius?" she asked. "I've never seen anyone as messy as she is. And her hair! It's always wild and sticking out all over."

Her mother laughed. "I don't know, Lydia," she said. "Maybe there's too much going on inside her head to pay attention to little details."

Lydia couldn't imagine what would make anyone not notice getting jelly in their hair, but it didn't seem worth arguing about. It was almost time for the bus. And she couldn't wait to talk to Jenna about the carnival!

The whole school seemed to vibrate with excitement as Lydia and Jenna got off the bus. They were putting their backpacks into their lockers when Marcia Hancock came up to them.

"Are you two going to the carnival tonight?" Marcia asked. "It's going to be really awesome."

Lydia glanced over at Jenna. Marcia loved to collect news. Unfortunately she also liked to share it with everyone she met, which was why they privately called her "The Mouth." Marcia had been trying for weeks to find out if Jenna liked Tom Bennett.

"We wouldn't miss it for anything," Lydia said. She gave her stuff one final shove and slammed the locker door shut before anything could escape.

"Well, I heard Tom Bennett talking about it," Marcia

15

said, lowering her voice so Jenna and Lydia had to step closer to listen. "He says he's sure to win at the balloon dart-toss. And he doesn't know what he'll do with the stuffed animal he'll win."

Marcia smiled slyly at Jenna. Jenna's face turned pink. She opened her mouth as if she was going to answer, but nothing came out. Lydia rushed to her friend's rescue.

"He's just bragging," Lydia said. "I've played that game before. It's not easy. You have to pop at least three balloons with four darts." She glanced at Jenna. "I doubt if Tom will have to worry about what to do with his prize." Jenna nodded her head in agreement.

Marcia looked disappointed. "I don't know," she said slowly. "He sounded pretty sure of himself."

"Oh, Marcia," Jenna said with a nervous laugh. "You know how boys are."

Marcia reluctantly agreed, then hurried off toward their homeroom. Jenna let out her breath in a whoosh.

"That was close," Jenna said. "I'd hate for The Mouth to tell the world I like Tom. Especially since I don't know if he likes me."

She grabbed Lydia's arm and squeezed it. "But if Tom won a stuffed animal for me I'd just die," Jenna added breathlessly. "I'd sleep with it always."

Lydia nodded, smiling for her friend's happiness even though her arm was feeling a bit numb. She couldn't help but think how lucky Jenna was. Not only was Jenna an only child, but she might be the first sixth-grade girl with a boyfriend. It wasn't fair. Even if she had a boyfriend, with her luck he'd win her a rubber snake!

She glanced over at her friend's dreamy smile. "Come down from the clouds, Jenna. It's time to go to class."

"I know," Jenna moaned as Lydia pulled her down the hall. "But I don't think I can survive until the carnival tonight."

Lydia wasn't sure she would survive either, but for different reasons. The class had a surprise math quiz from Mr. Henke, and math didn't add up for Lydia. Then Mr. Henke caught her passing a note from Sarah to Alison during social studies. He made her read it aloud, and Lydia could have died of embarrassment. The note said, "Mark Hartman is so cute." And Lydia didn't even like him!

Lunch wasn't much better than class. Brian Temple aimed the ketchup bottle at Cindy Williams—and hit Lydia instead. A bright red stain decorated the front of her shirt.

By the time Lydia got off the bus, the carnival was all she could think about. At least her terrible day would have a happy ending.

"What happened to you?" Katie asked, looking at Lydia's shirt as they got off the bus.

17

"I got in someone's way," Lydia muttered.

Katie grinned. "Just like you do at home."

Lydia stopped halfway through the kitchen door. "I get in the way?" she shouted. "I was here first! You're the one who gets in the way, squirt."

"Not quite," Mike said from his seat at the kitchen table. "I was here before either of you. Guess that gives me first rights." He bit into his sandwich, then continued talking around a mouthful of peanut butter. "What are we arguing about, anyway?"

"None of your business," Lydia said. She stooped down to pet Jake, who sat patiently by the table, waiting for stray crumbs to hit the floor.

"Lydia got in someone's way at school today, and I said it was just like at home," Katie told him. "She's a little grouchy tonight, so you better not say anything."

Katie looked at the peanut-butter jar, bottle of ketchup, and bologna packet lying on the table in front of Mike. "And you'd better not show her what you're eating either," she added.

Lydia stood up and glared at both of them. "I am not grouchy," she said loudly. "I am just tired of having food spilled on me. I'm tired of getting laughed at, wearing old clothes, and having everyone get into my things. And I am tired of being the one smooshed in the middle."

Mike stopped chewing and Katie stood perfectly still.

18

They stared at her. Lydia wondered if they thought she was crazy. They looked at her as if she had two heads.

Just then she felt something on her shoulder. She looked sideways into dark black eyes surrounded by bumpy green skin.

"Eeek!" she screamed, and jumped.

The green blob fell to the floor and started to hop. Mike and Katie burst into laughter as Erik stood in the doorway, grinning.

"What's wrong, Lyd? Don't ya like frogs?" Erik asked. He hurried across the room to catch his green friend before the dog got it.

Lydia's heartbeat pounded in her ears. "Not funny!" she yelled. "Will everyone just leave me alone!"

As she stomped off to her room, Lydia heard Erik say, "Gee, what a grouch."

CHAPTER 4

Lydia ignored everyone during supper, even though it wasn't easy.

Erik said, "What's that ugly thing on your shoulder, Lyd?"

And Mike answered, "That's just her head."

But she managed to pretend she hadn't heard them. The carnival would start soon, and she was determined to put her bad day behind her and have a good time.

After supper Lydia hurried to put on the red flowered dress. She looked in the mirror. It wasn't as nice as Jenna's dress, but with black leggings it wasn't too bad, she told herself. She did a ballerina twirl. The skirt flared out, swishing when she stopped. Maybe it would be all right.

The door opened and a curly head appeared in the opening. "Mom said to hurry up," Katie announced. "We're all ready to go."

She opened the door wider and looked at Lydia. "Is

that Sharon's old dress—the one you didn't want to wear?" Katie asked. "It's cute."

Lydia's smile faded. "You'll probably get your turn to wear it too," she muttered.

"That's okay," Katie said. "I like red."

Lydia wrinkled her nose as Katie turned and left the room. Katie was just a kid. If she were eleven she wouldn't want to wear Lydia's clothes any more than Lydia liked wearing Sharon's old stuff. Of course by the time Katie was older, Mom would probably give in to buying all new clothes every time Katie had to go somewhere! She sighed. If she couldn't be an only child, why couldn't she at least have been the youngest?

Sharon was leaving as Lydia stepped into the living room. "I'll be home by midnight," Sharon said before pulling the front door closed.

"Home from where?" Lydia's father asked, too late for Sharon to answer.

"You know, Dad," Mike said. He leaned against the door frame between the kitchen and living room. "She's doing the usual. Cheers, talking, flirting. Her mouth never stops."

"At least her mouth isn't always chewing," Lydia said. "I suppose you and Brian are going out for pizza."

"No, smartie, we're going bowling," Mike answered. He moved away from the doorway and headed for the back door. "We'll save the pizza for afterward."

21

"Well, don't you be late," Lydia's father said. He folded his newspaper and pushed himself from the recliner. "Guess we'd better get our show on the road too."

Lydia didn't mind having her parents come because it meant the two little pests would have to stay with them. She and Jenna would be free to explore the carnival on their own. It was going to be fabulous!

Jenna was waiting at the ticket booth, and Lydia rushed up to join her. They bought a handful of tickets for the games and started for the gymnasium, where the booths were set up.

"Meet us back here at eight-thirty," Lydia's mother called after them.

Lydia waved in acknowledgment. She wanted to get lost in the crowd before Katie tried to tag along. She grabbed Jenna's arm and pulled her into the sea of bodies.

"Whoa," Jenna said. "Slow down. Every family in Blooming Prairie must be here. It's jam packed."

The air vibrated with the thrum of voices. Faces shifted as the mass of bodies moved around the booths.

"Yeah," Lydia agreed. "It's even worse than my house." She grinned at Jenna. "Where to first?"

"Let's get our faces painted," Jenna said, pointing to a long table where several teachers and older kids were set up with paints and brushes. "At least we'll be out of the mob for a few minutes."

They went over to the table and waited their turn. Jenna chose a cluster of balloons for her cheek. Lydia got a unicorn head on hers.

Then they tried their luck at several game booths. Lydia won a lei of silk flowers by tossing a ball into a basket. She put it around her neck and grinned at Jenna.

"Do I look exotic, like a Hawaiian dancer?" she asked.

Jenna shook her head. "Maybe if you put on a grass skirt and did the hula. . . ."

The thought of trying the hula with all these people around made Lydia's face feel hot. "I think I'll wait," she said. "After all, you're the one who wants to catch someone's attention."

She gave Jenna's arm a nudge, and they both giggled. Tom Bennett had to be in the crowd somewhere. But Lydia wasn't sure Jenna really wanted to find him.

Just then Marcia Hancock came up with two other girls from their sixth-grade class. "I love your unicorn," Marcia said. She turned her face sideways to display a matching one.

"Thanks," Lydia said. "Yours is great too."

Marcia leaned over toward Jenna. "Want to go over to the balloon dart-toss? I saw Tom and Joe Caldwell heading over there a minute ago."

Jenna chewed on her lower lip. She looked over at Lydia and raised her eyebrows.

"Why not?" Lydia said, shrugging her shoulders. "Let's see if Tom's as good as he says he is."

The group maneuvered their way through the crowd and over to the dart-toss booth. Joe was just throwing his last dart.

"Nice try," Tom said as the dart bounced off a balloon without popping it.

Joe shrugged and picked up a key-ring prize for the balloon he had managed to pop. "Let's see what you can do, champ," he said to Tom.

Tom paid his ticket and took the four darts the man behind the counter held out to him. He glanced at the girls, then stared at the wall of balloons, shifting from foot to foot. The first dart hit a pink balloon. It popped.

"Yea," the girls cheered.

"Beginner's luck," Joe said with a grin.

Tom shifted his weight and tossed the second dart. The tattered remains of a blue balloon stuck to the wall.

"All right," Lydia said. She glanced at Jenna. Her friend looked like she was holding her breath. Lydia gave Jenna a nudge with her elbow so she wouldn't turn blue.

The third dart flew from Tom's hand and stuck in the wall, right next to a balloon. No one said a word. Lydia's palms felt like her dog had licked them. She rubbed her hands against the sides of her dress.

Tom held the last dart up, rocking it back and forth in the air. Lydia held her breath as he released it and watched it sail toward the wall. A green balloon popped.

"Yahoo," Joe yelled as he slapped Tom's shoulder.

Lydia felt like the Cheshire cat, grinning from ear to ear. Her hands were shaking—and she hadn't even been the one throwing the darts.

"We have a big winner," the man behind the counter said. "Pick a prize from the row of stuffed animals."

Lydia watched Tom glance sideways at Jenna. A crimson color crept up his neck as Tom's gaze met Jenna's. Lydia wondered if she'd ever make a boy blush like that. Not that she was sure she wanted to.

Tom picked a cuddly brown bear with a blue ribbon around its neck and moved away from the counter. "I need a soda," he announced. "It's getting hot in here."

Everyone followed Tom upstairs to the cafeteria and exchanged a ticket for a cup of soda.

"The game was rigged," Joe exclaimed with a grin. "That last balloon I hit should have popped."

"No way," Tom said. "My little sister could have thrown it harder than you did."

Lydia shook her head. Boys were always playing these macho games. Like it really mattered who could throw darts the best.

Then Marcia stepped between the boys and looked at Tom. "So Tom," she said, "what are you going to do with the bear you won?" Marcia glanced in Jenna's direction with a knowing smile.

Jenna was looking down at her shoes, but Lydia could tell she was biting her lip again. Marcia and her big mouth, Lydia thought angrily. Why couldn't she leave Jenna and Tom alone?

Suddenly a smile crept across Lydia's face. "You know," she said slowly, "the bear's ribbon matches Jenna's dress."

Tom glanced down at the bear. "You're right," he said. He looked back up at Jenna. "They match, so it must be Jenna's bear."

He thrust the bear out toward Jenna. She raised her head to look at it. "Thanks," Jenna mumbled. "I'll take good care of him."

Things couldn't have turned out better, Lydia told herself as she looked at Jenna holding the bear. Jenna smiled shyly, and Tom glowed his usual fire-engine red. It was perfect. Lydia was happy for her friend. Maybe the carnival wouldn't be a disaster like the rest of the day.

Then a whirlwind disrupted the scene. Actually two whirlwinds . . . named Katie and Erik.

"You should see the neat stuff we got," Katie said. Her curls bounced wildly as she ran up to Lydia. "See!

A decoder ring, and a high-bounce ball, and a whistle.''
She paused to blow shrilly through the yellow whistle.

Lydia clapped her hands over her ears. "Katie!" she
yelled over the noise.

"Wait till you see the cool pen I got," Erik said,
pushing his way into the crowd to stand in front of
Lydia. He pointed the pen at her. Blue ink shot out onto
the front of Lydia's dress.

"Erik!" Lydia shrieked. She looked down at the blue
stain. "You've ruined my dress!"

"It's okay," Erik said with a chuckle. He squirted
the pen onto his own shirt. "It's disappearing ink."

"Besides," Katie piped up, "you didn't like Sharon's
old dress, anyway."

Lydia wanted to disappear with the ink. Why was she
cursed with a little brother and sister?

"Hey, that's cool," Joe said to Erik. "Where'd you
get it?"

Erik started to tell the boys which booth to go to, but
Lydia couldn't listen. She was too embarrassed. She had
to get away. She ran toward the girls' rest room.

Lydia stood in front of the mirror, staring at her dress.
All that remained of the ink was a wet spot.

Jenna hurried into the rest room after Lydia. "It'll be
okay," Jenna said. "See, the spot is almost gone."

Lydia's lip trembled. She couldn't look at her friend.
"I thought I'd die right there," she whispered.

Jenna put her hand on Lydia's shoulder. "Everyone knows how little kids like to play jokes," Jenna told her. "Don't worry about it."

"It wasn't just Erik," Lydia groaned. "It was Katie telling everyone this is Sharon's old dress. It'll be all over school by morning."

Jenna looked confused. "Why?" she asked. "What does it matter if it's your sister's dress?"

Lydia shook her head. How could Jenna understand? She didn't have to wear hand-me-downs. And she didn't have to put up with younger siblings playing jokes on her. Jenna was so lucky Lydia could barely stand it.

"I should have worn my birthday dress, for the thirteenth time," Lydia muttered. "It couldn't have been any more of a disaster than this."

"Don't be silly," Jenna said. "What you wear doesn't matter to anyone."

"Oh, yeah," Lydia said, raising her eyebrows. "You might not be holding that bear if you hadn't worn your blue dress tonight."

The doubt and disappointment that flickered across Jenna's face made Lydia feel awful. She hadn't meant to ruin her friend's happiness just because she felt miserable.

"I'm sorry. I didn't mean it," Lydia reassured her. "Tom would have picked a bear that matched whatever you were wearing."

"Thanks," Jenna said. She hugged the bear. "I think I'll name him Benny."

Lydia stared at the bear. "You're really lucky, Jenna," she said flatly.

"But you're lucky too," Jenna told her. "Katie and Erik are crazy about you. That's why they were so excited to show you their stuff."

"That kind of luck I can live without," Lydia muttered. "You can have it."

Suddenly she grabbed Jenna's arm. "That's it," she shouted. "You can have them."

"What are you talking about?" Jenna asked. "Don't you think your parents would have something to say about me taking your little brother and sister?"

"You don't have to take them," Lydia said, her confidence growing as her idea took root in her head. "We'll switch places."

Jenna looked at Lydia's black hair and held out a lock of her own blond hair. "Don't you think they'd notice the difference?"

Lydia giggled. She knew it could work. "We can tell our parents it's an assignment for social studies," she explained. "To research how another family lives."

"I don't know," Jenna said slowly.

"Please, Jen," Lydia pleaded. "Just for a week?"

Jenna looked doubtful. Lydia did her best sad-eyed

29

puppy look, hoping to sway her. For a minute she was afraid Jenna would say no.

"Okay," Jenna said finally. "For one week I'll be Jenna Barnsworth."

"And I'll be Lydia Taylor," Lydia said happily. "It'll be great."

Lydia grinned, barely able to contain her excitement. One week of being an only child. It sounded wonderful. She'd have a room to herself. And best of all, no brothers or sisters to drive her crazy.

A week in heaven!

CHAPTER 5

Convincing her parents the next day was trickier than Lydia had thought it would be.

"It sounds like an interesting project," her mother said. "But don't they usually send a note home asking permission for something like this?"

Lydia gulped. She didn't like to lie to her parents. But this was just a little white one. And for a good cause—her sanity.

"Well, it's a volunteer project," she said carefully. "Just a few of us who have good friends to switch with are doing it. Then we'll report back to the rest of the class."

"I think it's a great idea," her father said. "Ben Taylor's a good man. He sends me a lot of loan customers at the bank from his real-estate business. Besides, you two girls are together so much, Jenna already seems like one of the family."

"That's true," Mom added, "and Jenna's mother is

very nice. She's asked me to sit in with her bridge club before.''

Mom looked at Lydia and Lydia held her breath. Please don't ask any more questions, she begged silently.

''I guess it would be okay,'' Mom said finally.

Lydia breathed a sigh of relief. ''Thanks, Mom. I think I'd better call Jenna and tell her right away.''

She hurried from the room before her parents could change their minds. Hopefully her parents wouldn't find out she and Jenna were the only volunteers. It was possible that they could. After all, Blooming Prairie wasn't very big. Her parents knew lots of people. But why would anyone be talking about a sixth-grade project?

Besides, she told herself firmly as she ignored a stab of guilt, a little privacy was worth the risk. She'd make it up to her parents eventually for the white lie.

''Jenna,'' Lydia whispered when her friend answered the phone, ''they bought it. We get to change places for a whole week.''

''That's great,'' Jenna said, but she didn't sound as enthusiastic as Lydia. ''My parents said okay too.''

''When can we switch?'' Lydia asked, hoping it could be right away.

''How about Sunday after dinner,'' Jenna said. ''My mom promised to take me to the movies tonight if I help with errands this afternoon.''

"All right," Lydia said, trying to keep the disappointment from her voice. She could put up with her siblings for another twenty-four hours when she'd be away from them for a whole week.

A week as an only child, Lydia thought dazedly as she hung up the phone. No one snooping through her things. No one arguing over which television program to watch. No frogs on her shoulder. It sounded like a dream. But if she was dreaming, she didn't want to wake up.

Lydia wandered into her bedroom. She stopped in the doorway.

"What are you doing?" she asked Katie.

Katie moved a dinosaur on the shelf and set an Indian teepee beside it. "Cleaning up," Katie said without looking at Lydia.

"You never clean up your junk," Lydia said suspiciously. "What's going on?"

Katie sat back on her heels and looked at Lydia. "I heard you talking to Mom about Jenna staying here. I don't want her to think I'm messy."

"But you are messy," Lydia said. "Anyway, Jenna's seen your mess a thousand times. Why is this any different?"

A smile crept slowly across Katie's face. "If Jenna's going to be my new big sister, I want her to be happy here. Maybe she'll like it and decide to stay."

33

Lydia's mouth fell open. It sounded like Katie wanted to get rid of her. After all the things she'd done for the little squirt, Lydia fumed silently. Well, she didn't care. She'd have a room to herself.

"It'll take a lot more than cleaning up your junk to make Jenna want to stay past a week with you," Lydia said smugly. She went out the door, leaving Katie to her cleaning.

Lydia wandered through the house, trying to decide what to do until Sunday. She didn't want to pack her things with Katie in the room. And Jenna was busy with her mother.

What did an only child do on a boring Saturday afternoon? she asked herself. Slowly Lydia smiled. Listen to music, of course. And she had Jenna's favorite Amy Hart release to listen to.

Mike was sitting at the coffee table when Lydia came into the family room. He had half the encyclopedias spread on the floor around him.

"Are you messing around or doing something serious?" Lydia asked.

"Depends on why you want to know," Mike answered. He stretched his shoulders as if he'd been sitting there too long.

"I wanted to listen to some music."

"Then it depends on what you want to listen to,"

Mike said with a grin. "If it's some of your classical junk, forget it."

Lydia made a face at him. "No, it's not Beethoven," she said. "It's one of Jenna's new albums."

"If it's Jenna's music, then go ahead and play it." Mike's grin widened. "Jenna has good taste."

"Meaning I don't?" Lydia asked, glaring at Mike.

"Take it however you want," Mike answered easily. "If Jenna's going to be here for a week, I might as well get used to her music."

"You sound pretty happy about it," Lydia said accusingly.

"Why not," Mike answered, his lips twitching as he tried to hide his smile. "We get rid of you for a week and get Jenna in your place. Maybe she'll appreciate my inspired creations."

"If you mean the awful junk you eat, don't count on it. Like you said, Jenna has good taste."

Lydia made another face at Mike and left the room, ignoring his laughter trailing behind her. She'd listen to Jenna's album some other time. Like when she had a room to herself and no brothers or sisters to drive her crazy.

Lydia was packed and ready to go early Sunday afternoon. She couldn't wait to begin her week as an only child. Mike had teased her all Saturday evening about

35

leaving for Jenna's house as soon as possible. Then Erik had joined in, showing her the door and asking why she didn't use it. Lydia had gone to bed early just to get away from them. But then Katie had mumbled in her sleep all night, keeping Lydia awake. Just as she had begun to doze, Sharon came home, and then her friends honked the car horn as they drove off. It had been practically dawn by the time Lydia had fallen asleep.

She carried her suitcase down to the living room. Her father was reading the Sunday paper.

"Dad, could you drive me over to Jenna's house?" Lydia asked. "I don't want to walk all that way with a suitcase."

Her father put down the paper. "I suppose I could. But are you going already? It's only two o'clock."

"Well, I want to get settled in," she told him. "I've got homework to do tonight."

"All right," he said as he stood up and smiled at her. "We're going to miss you, you know."

Lydia looked away. She didn't want to think about her parents missing her. She felt bad about her white lie, but what was worse was knowing she wouldn't miss anyone. It was going to be too exciting being the only kid in the house.

Mom came through the doorway from the kitchen. "Behave yourself at the Taylors'," she said. "And remember your manners."

"Yes, Mom," Lydia answered. She didn't know why her mother always seemed to think she'd forget her manners in public. It wasn't as if she were Katie. Still, it wasn't a good time to argue, so she merely smiled weakly.

"We'll miss you," her mother said, giving Lydia a big hug. She looked down at Lydia. "Guess you'll get to have your own room this week, just like you've been wanting."

Lydia felt her cheeks burn guiltily. She didn't know what to say. There was no denying her excitement at having a room to herself for a week. But this was supposed to be a school project. She didn't want to make her parents suspicious of what was going on by acting too happy.

Luckily Lydia didn't have to say anything. Her father picked up her suitcase and opened the door.

"Let's not make this into a long good-bye, Loretta," he said. "After all, she'll only be a few blocks away."

Lydia kissed her mother's cheek and gratefully followed her father out to the car. In a few minutes she was standing inside the Taylors' front door, grinning at Jenna.

"Are you ready to be Jenna Barnsworth?" Lydia asked.

"Sure," Jenna answered, smiling back at her. "It'll be fun being a big sister."

37

Lydia glanced over at Mrs. Taylor and added hastily, "And educational for our reports. Right, Jenna?"

Jenna nodded, a pink tinge staining her cheeks. "Right," she agreed.

Lydia's father picked up Jenna's suitcase. "We'll take good care of your daughter," he told Mrs. Taylor. "See you Friday, Lydia."

The door closed behind Jenna and Mr. Barnsworth. Lydia stared at the door for a moment. An odd queasiness settled in her stomach and her chest felt tight. But she didn't want to think about it. She wasn't a first-grader who had never been away from home before. She was a sixth-grader about to start a dream adventure. Maybe she was just over excited.

"Why don't you get settled," Mrs. Taylor told Lydia as she turned toward the hallway. "You know, you and Jenna have been friends for so long, I already think of you as our second daughter. So make yourself at home."

"Thanks," Lydia mumbled, feeling suddenly awkward. It was strange to be at Jenna's without Jenna.

She picked up her suitcase and moved toward Jenna's room. Her room, she reminded herself, for one entire, wonderful week.

CHAPTER 6

The alarm went off too early the next morning. Lydia felt as though she'd barely slept. Jenna should get a softer bed, she thought grumpily.

After she'd washed her face and gotten dressed, Lydia felt a little better. She grabbed her backpack and schoolbooks from where she'd put them on Jenna's desk and went out to the kitchen.

Mrs. Taylor was at the stove, dressed in a pink fuzzy robe and slippers. Lydia's eyes widened. There were rabbit heads on Mrs. Taylor's feet.

"I hope you like scrambled eggs," Mrs. Taylor said.

Lydia sat down at the table and forced a smile. She didn't know if her stomach was awake enough for eggs. She usually had cold cereal before school. But she didn't want to hurt Mrs. Taylor's feelings.

"That sounds great," she said.

Mr. Taylor sat at the table drinking coffee and reading the newspaper. He looked around the edge of the paper.

"Good morning, Lydia," he said briskly. "If you'd like to read the comics section, I'm finished with it."

Lydia blinked. Reading at the table wasn't allowed at home because her mother said it was rude. Was a rule still a rule when she wasn't at home?

"That's all right," Lydia answered. "I'll just eat my eggs. I don't want to be late for the bus."

Things certainly were different at the Taylors' house, Lydia told herself as she pushed scrambled eggs around on her plate. She wondered if Jenna was disappointed to be eating cold cereal.

The bus stopped at Jenna's house before it went by the Barnsworths' house. Lydia sat in their usual seat, waiting for Jenna. She nibbled on a fingernail and hoped Katie hadn't kept Jenna awake all night with her mumbling. Jenna might demand they switch back, and Lydia wasn't ready to go home yet.

Jenna and Katie climbed into the bus at their stop. They were giggling and whispering as they came down the aisle. Lydia couldn't believe her eyes.

"What happened to Katie's hair?" Lydia asked. She stared at the soft, fluffy curls neatly framing Katie's face. This wasn't her little sister, the junior Albert Einstein!

Katie and Jenna both sat down in the seat with Lydia. "Isn't it gorgeous," Jenna said, beaming like a proud parent.

"Jenna fixed my hair," Katie said happily. "She even put hair spray on it."

Lydia looked from one smiling face to the other. Katie hated having her hair combed. And she always said hair spray stunk. But it did look nice for a change.

"It looks great," Lydia mumbled grudgingly, annoyed with herself that Katie's hairdo bothered her. "Hope you can keep it that way all day."

"I will," Katie said confidently. She looked up at Jenna like a puppy wanting to be petted. "Will you fix my hair again tomorrow, Jenna?"

"Sure. It was fun."

Jenna smiled at Katie, and Lydia turned toward the window, feeling slightly nauseous. Whether it was the happy pair next to her or the eggs from breakfast rebelling in her stomach, she wasn't sure. It was going to be a long ride to school.

As soon as the bus stopped at Forest Hills, Lydia grabbed her bag and stood up. Jenna and Katie had laughed all the way to school about Erik's latest project demolishing the family-room phone. They hadn't even noticed Lydia's lack of enthusiasm.

When Katie went into her second-grade classroom, Lydia breathed a sigh of relief.

"You know, Jenna," Lydia said, "if Katie gets on your nerves just tell her to bug off. Just because you're sharing a room doesn't mean you have to baby-sit the squirt.''

Jenna frowned at Lydia. "I like Katie. It's fun having a little sister.''

Wait until the little sister snoops through her things, Lydia thought. Then it won't be so much fun.

But Lydia didn't have a chance to say anything. Marcia Hancock hurried down the hall to meet them.

"How's your bear, Jenna?'' Marcia asked. "Everyone is talking about how Tom won it for you.''

Lydia and Jenna glanced at each other. Lydia rolled her eyes in a circle.

"And how does everyone know about it?'' Jenna asked in a disgusted tone.

Marcia shrugged. "You know how word gets around,'' she said innocently. "And everyone loves a romance.''

"A romance,'' Jenna squeaked.

Lydia couldn't help but smile. Jenna had gotten Tom's attention—and everyone else's too. Maybe trading places had switched their luck. And if she had Jenna's good luck, she could hardly wait to try it out.

Marcia grinned and patted Jenna on the shoulder. "Don't worry. I'll tell everyone how it happened.''

As Marcia hurried away, Jenna muttered, "That's what I'm afraid of.''

She turned toward Lydia. "Marcia's stories never come close to what actually happened. By lunchtime everyone will probably be talking about how Tom gave me Benny as a token of his undying love. And by the time school is out, we'll be engaged—with a bear!''

Lydia laughed out loud. "Just think about poor Tom. He'll be as red as a beet all day."

Jenna glared at Lydia and started to open her mouth. But the warning bell sounded and they had to hurry to stow their bags before class. Mr. Henke loved to give tardy slips to students who weren't seated before the second bell.

Lydia barely made it to her seat in time. She was still grinning, thinking up sequels in her head for Jenna's romance story, when math class started.

"Today we're going to work with fractions," Mr. Henke announced. "I'll show you a few examples on the board, and then you'll work the problems on page fifty in your book."

The smile faded from Lydia's face. Fractions! She thought story problems were hard, but fractions were even worse.

By the time the class had to close their math books and start with spelling, Lydia had two problems done. The page Mr. Henke had assigned had twenty problems. She'd be up all night trying to get them finished. What a way to start her week as an only child, Lydia thought with a groan.

At lunch Lydia joined Jenna at the table where the

sixth-grade girls always sat. She set down her tray and plopped onto the seat.

"I'll never finish all those math problems tonight," Lydia moaned. "Did you get them done?"

Jenna shook her head. "No way. I'll be working on them all evening."

"Great," Lydia exclaimed. "You can come over and we'll do them together."

"But I promised your mom I'd watch Katie and Erik tonight while she goes to the PTA meeting," Jenna said. "Why don't you come over to my house?"

"I live at your house," Lydia said with a giggle.

Jenna nudged her arm. "You know what I mean."

Lydia thought about it a minute. She didn't want to go home yet, but it might be fun to visit. Maybe her family would treat her like a guest. She could just imagine Katie cleaning the room for her. And Mike trying to eat like a civilized person.

"Okay," Lydia agreed. "I'll come over after supper."

Suddenly Lydia heard a commotion at the tables behind her. She turned around to see what was going on. Several sixth-grade boys were huddled in a circle. Tom Bennett stood in the middle, with Joe Caldwell nearby. And, of course, Marcia hovered around the outer edge of the circle.

As a red-faced Tom pushed his way out of the group

and headed for the door, Lydia heard one of the boys yell after him.

"Aren't you going to say hi to your girlfriend?"

The boys snickered loudly and Lydia glanced over at Jenna. She was staring down at her lunch like she'd never seen a sandwich before.

"What do you think that was all about?" Lydia whispered. "Tom looked awful mad."

"He's probably getting the same kind of teasing I've been getting all day," Jenna said miserably. "Tom must wish he'd never given me Benny."

Lydia wanted to reassure her friend that Tom wouldn't care what the guys said because he really liked her. But she couldn't look Jenna in the eye and say it. From the glow of his face when he'd left the cafeteria, Lydia was pretty sure Tom did care. And she knew she would hate to be the one everyone was talking about.

"So what if they tease," Lydia muttered, hoping she sounded more confident than she felt. "They're just jealous because Tom likes you."

Jenna didn't answer. Lydia sighed. So what if everyone was talking about Jenna and Tom? Jenna had everything she could wish for.

"You're really lucky, Jenna," Lydia said quietly.

Jenna frowned at her. "I don't feel lucky right now."

"Well you are," Lydia insisted. "Tom likes you, you

have your own room, a closet full of clothes, your own stereo.''

Lydia paused to catch her breath. She could go on and on about how lucky Jenna was.

Jenna shook her head. ''Those things aren't important,'' Jenna said angrily. ''It can get pretty lonely sitting in your room, listening to music all by yourself. Like being all dressed up with nowhere to go.''

It was Lydia's turn to shake her head. ''You're crazy,'' she told Jenna. ''It's easy to say those things aren't important when you have them all. But I can't wait to crank on the stereo after school and be all by myself.''

''Well, enjoy yourself,'' Jenna said. She looked at Lydia and frowned again. ''Some people are lucky and don't even know it.''

Lydia's eyebrows drew together into a straight line across her forehead. What was that supposed to mean? She couldn't imagine what Jenna was talking about.

CHAPTER 7

Lydia rushed into her new room after the bus dropped her off at the Taylors'. She couldn't wait to turn on Jenna's stereo and have the whole room to herself. She could lie on the bed and write in her journal without a snoopy little sister wanting to see what she was doing. It would be wonderful.

When the first album was over, Lydia turned the stereo off. Jenna's music certainly sounded different when it was the only sound in the room. She wandered around the room and touched a ceramic doll sitting on the wall shelf, its pink lacy dress flowing primly down to her feet. Jenna had a beautiful collection of dolls and rows of furry creatures sitting neatly in their places.

Jenna's room was always so neat and tidy that Lydia was afraid to touch anything. Even now, when it was supposed to be her room, she was afraid to mess it up. Then Jenna would be mad they switched places. Of course, Jenna didn't have to worry about Lydia's room. With Katie around it was always a mess.

Lydia thought momentarily about working on her math but quickly dismissed the idea. It would be more fun to do it tonight with Jenna. She opened the bedroom door and wandered out into the kitchen.

"Hi," Mrs. Taylor said as Lydia came into the room. "How was school today?"

Lydia walked over to the counter where Mrs. Taylor was working on supper. "Okay, but we had these terrible fraction problems in math. It's not exactly my favorite subject," she confided.

"Mine neither," Mrs. Taylor said with a laugh, "but Jenna is pretty good with numbers. She takes after her father."

"I know," Lydia agreed. "In fact, I'm going over after supper to work on my math homework with her. If anyone can help me understand it, it's Jenna."

Mrs. Taylor smiled sympathetically. "I'm sure you'll get it. And I'm glad you're going over to see Jenna tonight. I have to go to the PTA meeting, and Ben is meeting some clients tonight. I'd hate to leave you all alone."

Part of Lydia wanted to protest that she'd be fine by herself, but another part was glad she wouldn't have to stay alone. With her big family she was never the only one home.

"I'll drop you off when I go to the meeting and pick you up afterward," Mrs. Taylor said.

Lydia nodded. She couldn't help but wonder how often Jenna stayed by herself. It would be awfully quiet. Like a graveyard, Lydia thought with a shiver. And Jenna didn't even have a dog like Jake to keep her company.

Lydia set the table and helped Mrs. Taylor finish cooking. It didn't seem like a lot of food as she set it out, but of course there were only three people. And Mike wasn't one of them. He counted for two people at the supper table.

By the time Mrs. Taylor dropped Lydia off, there were butterflies dancing in her stomach. It was silly to get excited about visiting her own family, Lydia scolded herself. But the butterflies weren't listening.

Lydia stopped at the front door. Should she ring the doorbell? That seemed even sillier than the butterflies. Before she could decide, the front door jerked open.

"We don't want any," Erik yelled. Then he slammed the door shut. Lydia could hear the howl of Erik's laughter from the other side of the door.

The butterflies flew out the window. Lydia pounded on the door with her fist. "Open this door right now, Erik Barnsworth!" she shouted. Under her breath she added, "You little brat."

The door swung open again and Erik stood there, giving Lydia an angelic smile. "Did you want something?"

"You know I did," Lydia said as she strode past him into the living room. "Where's Jenna?"

"In the family room doing homework," Erik said with disgust. Suddenly he brightened. "Would you like to build a space station with me, Lyd? I traded Jonathan a Ninja turtle for a neat rocket ship."

Lydia looked down at Erik. His bright blue eyes and tousled sandy hair added to the appealing look on his face. Helping with one of Erik's creations would be a lot more fun than doing math. But she'd be in trouble with Mr. Henke if she didn't get her work finished.

"Sorry, I've got homework to do," Lydia told him.

"No one ever wants to play with me," Erik muttered.

He looked so forlorn that Lydia forgot about his slamming the door shut on her. She reached over and ruffled his hair. "Maybe next time I will."

Erik grinned at her. "An' I promise next time I won't shut the door on you."

Lydia laughed and shook her head. Erik was almost as good at keeping his promises as he was at putting things back together.

She walked down the hall and into the family room. Katie was sitting on the sofa, reading a book. Jenna sat on the floor by the coffee table.

"Have you got them all figured out?" Lydia asked hopefully, moving over to the table and setting her books down.

"I don't know," Jenna moaned. "Every time I think I'm getting the hang of it, the next one is different."

"You'll get it," Lydia said confidently. "Even your mom was bragging about what a math whiz you are."

Jenna glared at Lydia. "Maybe I'm all whizzed out."

Lydia would have started laughing if it hadn't been for the serious look on Jenna's face. Her friend was in no mood for joking around.

"Maybe I could try them," Katie volunteered. "I'm pretty good at math."

Lydia smothered a giggle as she watched Jenna's reaction. Jenna didn't look too thrilled to have a little sister at the moment.

"Get real," Jenna muttered. "Sixth-grade stuff is much harder than the simple add and subtract junk you second-graders get."

"Yeah, this stuff is murder," Lydia agreed. Of course she wasn't going to tell Jenna that Katie was in advanced math classes at school and could probably catch on quicker than either of them.

Lydia flipped open her math book to page fifty and picked up her pencil. "Let's see if I can get lucky and figure this out."

For half an hour Lydia struggled over the page of problems, comparing notes with Jenna on the ones she had done. Some of their answers matched, but on the ones where they were different, Lydia wasn't sure whose answer was right. Probably neither of them!

She was ready to give up when Mike came home from playing chess at his friend's house.

"Is the week up already?" Mike asked jokingly when he saw Lydia, "or do you just miss us so much you can't stay away?"

"Neither," Lydia muttered. "It's Mr. Henke and his fractions. He's going to flunk me out of sixth grade."

"Fractions!" Mike exclaimed. "They're a breeze. You should try geometry. Now there's something to cry about."

"Lydia's right," Jenna said. "Common denominators don't make sense."

Mike looked at Jenna and Lydia. Suddenly his smile disappeared. "Would you like some help?" he asked.

Lydia stared at her older brother. Mike offering help instead of jokes? She had to be in the wrong house. But Jenna was smiling up at Mike.

"Would we ever!" Jenna cried. "Look at problem fifteen and see if you can figure it out."

Mike sat down on the floor between them and looked at the book. "Hmmm. Didn't Mr. Henke tell you the trick?"

"I knew there had to be a trick," Lydia exclaimed. "He always waits a day to see if we can figure it out. Then he tells us the easy way, after we've gone crazy."

52

"He's a good teacher," Mike said with a laugh. "He's just trying to stretch your brain a bit."

"My brain doesn't like to be stretched," Lydia complained. She looked at Mike suspiciously. "Are you going to tell us the trick? Or are you trying to turn my brain into taffy too?"

"I don't know," Mike said slowly. "A taffy brain might be an improvement."

"A taffy brain is better than a peanut-butter brain any day," Lydia replied. She started to add something about his gross peanut-butter sandwiches when Jenna interrupted.

"Will you two stop it," Jenna demanded. She looked reproachfully at Mike. "I thought you were going to help us." Then Jenna turned to Lydia. "And if you'd stop fighting with him, maybe we could learn how to do these stupid problems."

Lydia's face felt hot. Jenna was right. Mike couldn't help them if she kept fighting with him. Maybe that was why he'd never helped her with her homework before.

She swallowed hard against the dryness in her throat. "Mike, would you please explain the trick to doing the problems?" she asked quietly.

Lydia could feel Mike's gaze on her face, but she couldn't bring her head up to meet his eyes. She had hoped her family would treat her like a guest. But she hadn't acted like one. She had fought and argued just like she did when she was at home.

Relief surged through her as Mike spoke. "The trick is to multiply each fraction by the bottom number, or denominator, of the other fraction," he said patiently. "Here, I'll show you what I mean."

The three of them worked on the problems for another half hour. When they were finished, Lydia leaned back and smiled. "You're right, Mike. Those aren't so bad once you know the trick."

"Or else I'm just a fantastic teacher," he said, grinning widely at Lydia.

Lydia looked over at Jenna and rolled her eyes toward the ceiling. "Watch out," she told Jenna. "Now he'll have an even bigger head."

Secretly Lydia couldn't help but think that Mike was a surprisingly good teacher. Not that she'd ever tell him, of course.

"All that teaching made me hungry," Mike announced. "Anyone want to join me for a peanut butter, tomato, bacon, and mayo sandwich?"

"Ick," Jenna groaned. "No way."

On second thought, Lydia told herself with a smile, he was still the same big brother.

CHAPTER 8

By the time Mrs. Taylor was due to arrive, Lydia couldn't wait to leave. Mike had turned back into his usual gross self after being so helpful. Then Katie had refused to leave the bedroom when Lydia and Jenna had wanted to talk, pointing out that it was her room too and she could be there if she wanted.

The final insult came when Lydia had rushed to answer the doorbell and tripped over Erik's space station in the living-room entryway. Instead of feeling sorry for her scraped hands and knees, all Erik could think about was his wrecked lunar landing.

"You wrecked it!" Erik yelled. "You ruin't my station one afore I made number two."

"What about me?" Lydia reminded him. "I've got gouges from your stupid building blocks. Why do you put your junk in everybody's way?"

"Junk!" Erik shrieked. "It was my bestest space-port."

"Will you quit arguing and answer the door," Jenna said over the commotion. She stood in the doorway to the living room and frowned at Lydia. "For gosh sakes, Lydia, he didn't do it on purpose."

Before Lydia could reach the door or tell Jenna what she thought of having her best friend side with her brat brother, the front door opened. Mr. and Mrs. Barnsworth walked into the room followed by Mrs. Taylor. They stopped inside the room and surveyed the mess.

"No blood," Mr. Barnsworth commented. "From the screams we heard outside, I expected blood and broken bones."

"And poor Mrs. Taylor standing there ringing the doorbell as we drove up. She probably wonders what kind of madhouse she's sent her daughter into," Lydia's mother said.

Of course, both of her parents looked at Lydia as if it were all her fault. They seemed to have forgotten that Jenna was the baby-sitter—and Lydia was the guest!

Jenna's mother laughed and patted Mrs. Barnsworth's arm. "Don't worry about it, Loretta. I think this is a great experience for Jenna. And having grown up in a family of four kids, I thought everything sounded pretty normal."

Lydia's mother smiled gratefully. "Thanks. Sometimes I'm not so sure."

"It's all Lydia's fault," Erik complained. "Jenna was

a good baby-sitter. Lydia isn't even supposed to live here anymore.''

Lydia gritted her teeth and kept her mouth shut to keep from remarking that she didn't want to be here either. All she wanted was to get out the door and go back to being an only child. If Jenna was so great, she could have the little monster forever.

"It wasn't all Lydia's fault, Erik," Jenna said. "She didn't mean to trip on your space station. After all, you did have it sort of in the way."

But Erik wasn't listening, and Lydia didn't feel like forgiving him or Jenna right then anyway. She edged toward the front door, hoping for a fast getaway.

"Sorry to keep you waiting, Mrs. Taylor," she said. "I've got everything ready to go."

"No problem." Jenna's mother smiled at Lydia and then glanced toward Jenna. "Did you two get your math problems finished?"

"Oh, yeah," Lydia said. She glanced over to where Mike was leaning against the door frame. "We had a little help."

Quickly she turned away, gave her parents each a good-night kiss on the cheek, and was out the door before Mike could come up with a smart-aleck remark. Jenna could thank him if she wanted. After all, Lydia told herself, Mike had never offered to help her with homework, just Jenna.

But even as she followed Mrs. Taylor to the car, she couldn't help but wonder if he'd offer to help her next time she had a taffy-brain math teaser.

Seeing Mrs. Taylor in bunny slippers didn't seem as strange to Lydia the second morning. But a hot breakfast still didn't appeal to her sleepy stomach like a bowl of cold cereal did. This morning breakfast was toasted waffles and sausage links. Lydia wondered for a minute what Mrs. Taylor would think if she asked for ice cream to cool off the waffles, but decided she didn't want her substitute mother to think she ate meals as strange as her brother Mike.

"I've got a favor to ask," Mrs. Taylor said while Lydia cut up her waffles into bite-sized squares and pretended it was a new type of cereal. "My bridge club meets here tonight, and I'd really appreciate if you could help me like Jenna usually does."

"Sure," Lydia said, momentarily forgetting about the sugar she was dumping on her food. "What do I have to do?"

"Oh, help with the food, set things out, serve coffee. Those sort of things. It's not hard. Jenna plays hostess for me so I can concentrate on my cards with the rest of the ladies."

"Sounds fun," Lydia said.

"I usually pay Jenna four dollars an hour. Does that sound okay?"

Lydia almost choked on her bite of waffle cereal. "Sure. Sounds great."

Mrs. Taylor smiled and placed another waffle onto Lydia's plate. "Why don't you ask Jenna if you can borrow one of her fancy dresses for tonight? I'm sure you can find one in her closet that you'd like to wear."

She had to be dreaming. A paid job *and* her pick of Jenna's clothes to wear? Lydia barely managed to nod her head in agreement.

"Great," Mrs. Taylor said. "Then I'll see you after school to work on the food."

Lydia didn't even think about what she was eating after that. She was too excited. This was her chance to show how grown-up she was, without Katie or Erik around to mess things up. She'd be the center of attention, serving the ladies just like a real waitress. It had to be more fun than taking care of Katie and Erik like Jenna had done last night.

When Jenna and Katie joined Lydia on the bus later, she was too excited to notice whether they were still being buddies. All she could think about was her chance to be a waitress—and to get paid for it.

"Guess what, Jenna," she said, then continuing before her friend could guess. "I'm going to be the waitress tonight for your mother's bridge party."

Jenna looked like she'd lost her favorite CD or ruined her best dress. "She's having the bridge party and I'm going to miss it?" Jenna wailed.

Lydia nodded, her grin stretching wide across her face. "I get to fill in for you. After all," she said brightly, "I am Lydia Taylor this week."

Jenna's delicate features drew together in a pout. "You'll have a great time," she said gloomily. "I always dress up like a waitress and pretend it's a coffee shop I'm working in. Some of the ladies even leave me a tip."

"Wow," Katie exclaimed from her spot on the other side of Jenna. "How much do you get?"

The glare Jenna gave Katie made Lydia feel sorry for her little sister. Katie couldn't help it if her curiosity always got the best of her. Besides, Lydia had wanted to ask the same thing.

"It's not the money that's important," Jenna said stiffly. "It's fun. Like having a real job."

Lydia exchanged glances with Katie, a silent agreement passing between them. It might be a fun job, but getting paid for it was even better.

When Lydia got to the Taylors' house after school, she raced upstairs to the bedroom. She couldn't wait to go through Jenna's closet to pick an outfit to wear. Even though Jenna hadn't been happy about missing the bridge party, she had suggested that Lydia borrow an outfit before Lydia could even ask. She felt like Cinderella. And tonight was the big event!

It took her a while to make a decision. The bed was littered with dresses, skirts, and blouses of every color and texture. But Lydia was finally satisfied. The pink dress she had chosen had a white lace pinafore covering the front, with long ties forming a big bow in the back. It was too old-fashioned to wear to school, but it looked to Lydia like what a waitress in a fancy restaurant would wear.

She stood in front of Jenna's full-length mirror and studied herself from every angle. If she pulled her long dark hair up at the back of her head, she'd look at least sixteen. Lydia rummaged through Jenna's vanity for pins to hold her hair in place. When she had finished, she smiled with satisfaction. She was ready to be the one and only hostess with the mostest.

Lydia started for the door, then turned back to look at the room. It looked like a cyclone had hit it. Jenna would have a fit, she thought guiltily. It was a good thing she had the rest of the week to clean it up before Jenna saw it again.

When Lydia entered the kitchen, Mrs. Taylor looked up from the tray of food she was working on. "Why, Lydia!" Mrs. Taylor exclaimed. "You look so grown-up I hardly recognized you."

Lydia felt the heat rushing to her cheeks, and she smiled shyly at Mrs. Taylor. "Thank you. I'll try to be a good waitress for you."

"You'll be just fine," Mrs. Taylor assured her. "All you have to do is serve coffee and tea, then bring in the trays of hors d'oeuvres."

Lydia squinted at the strange-colored mounds on the tray in front of Mrs. Taylor. Some were pale pink, some were orangeish, and some were a color she only saw when she got sick. Worse yet, Mrs. Taylor was adding strange specs of red, green, or black on top of them.

"Umm . . . is there something I can do to help with these uh . . ." Lydia's voice faded away. She didn't want to sound dumb, but she didn't have the faintest idea what to call those awful hunks of gunk.

"Sure," Mrs. Taylor said. "You can finish these for me." She pointed at a pink mound. "These are salmon paté. Put a green or black olive on them."

Her index finger moved to hover over an orange mound. "These are red snapper. I thought we'd add pimento."

Finally she indicated the ones that Lydia could scarcely bare to look at. "These are my specialty, trout mousse. Add whatever you want or leave them plain. They're wonderful."

Mrs. Taylor picked up an unadorned mousse mound

on a cracker and popped it into her mouth. She closed her eyes and murmured her approval.

Lydia stepped back a pace, just in case Mrs. Taylor's stomach thought differently of the tidbit. If these were the kind of snacks Jenna had to eat, maybe surviving a hot breakfast each morning wasn't so bad. Just the thought of eating a cracker with a strange mound of gunk on it was enough to make Lydia want to barf.

"Try one of each if you want," Mrs. Taylor said. "I always make more than we need, and tonight I even made a spinach dip."

Lydia struggled not to gag. She looked away from the tray of mounds and her gaze found the green-and-white spinach dip. Right then, chips with her mother's sour cream–and–soup mix dip seemed heavenly to Lydia.

"Thanks for the offer, but I had a big lunch at school," she said. "I don't think I could eat another thing."

Luckily Mrs. Taylor didn't insist.

After they finished the food, she and Jenna's mother checked the house. It was spotless and smelled like pine trees from the aerosol Mrs. Taylor had sprayed everywhere. But Mrs. Taylor still bustled around the room, straightening chairs and swiping at nonexistent dust while Lydia set out stacks of plates and napkins. They had just finished when the doorbell rang. Lydia

63

smoothed the lacy apron of her pinafore, then hurried to answer the door.

"Why, Jenna, you've changed since I last saw you," Mrs. Whitton exclaimed as Lydia opened the door. She smiled and patted Lydia on the shoulder, her bracelets jangling with the movement. "But you still look very nice, sweetie."

Lydia held the door while Mrs. Whitton strode into the hall. The perfume that lingered as Mrs. Whitton passed by made Lydia's nose twitch. It smelled like something had died. She held her breath but had already inhaled the stench. What she needed was fresh air.

She yanked the door open as two other ladies came up the walk toward the house. One of the ladies was Tony Adams's mother, another sixth-grader in her class. And, unfortunately, Mrs. Adams knew her.

Lydia's mouth went dry and her knees shook. She dreaded explaining why she was at the Taylors'. Blooming Prairie wasn't like Columbia or St. Louis. In their small town, everyone knew their neighbors, and worse yet, what their neighbors were doing.

"Aren't you the Barnsworth girl in my son Tony's class?" Mrs. Adams asked. "You look just like your mother."

Lydia nodded and ushered the ladies into the dining room. She hadn't realized how risky and embarrassing being the center of attention would be. Was this how

Jake felt when someone patted him on the head and called him a good dog—and he'd just chewed up a shoe in the next room?

After all the ladies had gathered in the dining room, Mrs. Taylor introduced her. "Jenna's best friend, Lydia, is our hostess tonight. The girls are trading places for a week as a class project in social studies."

"What a good idea!" Mrs. Whitton exclaimed.

"Yes," Mrs. Adams added. "I wonder why my son Tony never mentioned it. He'd love to get away from his little sister for a week."

Lydia felt the collar of her dress grow tight, and she tried not to fidget as she answered. "It was voluntary. Tony, um, must not have been interested."

While Mrs. Adams murmured in agreement, Lydia excused herself to the kitchen. Keeping up the pretense of a class project wasn't getting easier. It was like digging a hole, and if she dug any deeper she'd be in China.

Lydia made a silent promise to be a fantastic waitress tonight, a perfect houseguest the remainder of the week, and a model daughter the rest of her life. All she asked was to get through the evening without having to answer any more questions or tell any more lies. She'd bet her cheeks already had permanent red spots on them from the guilt.

Her first promise wasn't as easy to keep as she'd thought it would be. She asked each of the eight ladies what they wanted to drink. Then she had to remember who had wanted coffee and who had asked for tea.

Her hands shook as she served the drinks, and a little of Mrs. Adams's coffee sloshed into the saucer. At least it hadn't landed in Mrs. Adams's lap, but a dark stain dribbled down the front of Jenna's white pinafore.

Oh no, Lydia groaned silently. What if this was one of Jenna's favorite outfits? If the stain didn't come out, she'd owe Jenna a new dress. And she didn't think Jenna would want one of Sharon's hand-me-downs. There went all the money she'd earn tonight.

Careful not to get more stains on the dress, Lydia brought the first tray of hors d'oeuvres to the table. They disappeared instantly. She could hardly believe it. She'd have thought she was serving Mike and some of his friends.

Lydia looked over at Mrs. Taylor. "Should I bring in the other tray?" she asked.

"That would be wonderful, dear," Mrs. Taylor said. "We could also use some cream for our coffee."

"And sugar," Mrs. Adams said, smiling widely at the other ladies around the table. "My sweet tooth always insists on something."

Lydia nodded and hurried through the swinging door to the kitchen. Hors d'oeuvres, cream, and sugar. How was she going to carry it all? If Katie was around, Lydia could talk her into helping with the hors d'oeuvres tray.

And even if she couldn't trust Mike to carry food, she could always count on one of her siblings being around to lend a hand when she needed one.

But if Jenna managed by herself, so would she, Lydia thought with a confidence she didn't feel. Carefully she scooted the strange mounds over to one side of the tray. Then she found the sugar bowl and got the creamer from the refrigerator, where Mrs. Taylor had left it. She deposited the bowl and creamer in the area she'd cleared on the tray. Taking a deep breath, Lydia cautiously lifted the tray.

It felt a little lopsided, but she was determined to make it in one trip, and without any help. She'd just pretend she was walking while balancing a book on her head. She'd seen her older sister doing that when Sharon had thought no one was watching. Hopefully she wouldn't look as stiff and silly as Sharon had.

Slowly she moved toward the swinging door separating the kitchen and the dining room. The creamer jiggled dangerously, and she paused for it to settle down. Maybe she should make two trips, Lydia thought hesitantly. She drew a steadying breath. No, she could do it, she told herself firmly.

Pushing her hip carefully against the door, Lydia scooted through, giving the door a final nudge with her foot. She paused a moment to adjust the balance of the tray. Just as she started to step forward, the door swung back. It smacked her backside with a jarring thump and hit her elbow—right on her funnybone. Lydia lurched forward.

Hors d'oeuvres, cream, and sugar went flying through the air. Orange and pink mounds sailed like flying saucers invading the bridge party. A mound of mousse landed on Mrs. Whitton's shoulder. The cracker from a pink lump stuck on Mrs. Taylor's head while the pink mush slid slowly down her hair. A second chunk splattered across Mrs. Taylor's cheek as more of the invaders landed on the cards spread across the table.

The creamer spewed like a volcano across the blue carpet, erupting with a flow of white liquid. It rippled forward like a wave of lava, until it splashed against a lady's foot.

And the sugar flew through the air until it sprinkled down like fairy dust on Mrs. Adams's head.

Lydia groaned silently and wished she'd broken a leg in her fall. Then she'd at least get a little sympathy, since the way things were going, she sure wasn't going to get much of a tip tonight.

CHAPTER 9

Lydia was still groaning to herself when the alarm went off the next morning. How could she face Mrs. Taylor? She'd managed to slip up to her room last night before the party was over. Would Jenna's mom yell at her this morning?

And what about Jenna? Lydia put her head under the pillow as if to hide from the day. Her friend was sure to ask how hosting the bridge party had gone.

When she finally rolled out of bed, Lydia shook her head in disgust. Jenna had said it would be fun. Some fun. Taking care of Erik and Katie was better than being a juggling act for a group of women.

Her mood hadn't improved by the time the bus stopped at the Barnsworth house to pick up Jenna and Katie. Lydia curled up in the corner of the seat by the window, feeling sorry for herself. Mrs. Taylor hadn't said a word at breakfast about the bridge-party disaster. If Lydia had really been her daughter, Mrs. Taylor probably would have yelled at her like she deserved. But a substitute kid wasn't worth yelling at.

The seat bench creaked as the bus lurched into motion.

"So how did it go?" Jenna asked.

"Yeah," Katie said. "How much did you get?"

Lydia fought against the stinging behind her eyelids. She hung her head and mumbled, "I got what I deserved. Nothing."

Jenna's eyebrows went up. "Nothing? But the ladies are usually so generous," she said.

"Not when the hors d'oeuvres attack them," Lydia muttered.

"What!" Jenna exclaimed.

Lydia could feel the awful heat rising up her neck, but she forced herself to look at her friend. "I stumbled and the food landed on the table. And on your mother and her friends," she added ruefully.

Jenna's mouth fell open in astonishment and her face grew pale. "You ruined Mom's bridge party? Lydia, how could you!"

Lydia winced at her friend's words. She felt bad enough about what had happened. Couldn't Jenna be a little more sympathetic? It wasn't as though she'd done it on purpose.

Then Katie leaned forward in the seat and grinned

widely. "Wow—a food fight. I wish I could have been there."

A smile tugged at Lydia's mouth. It *had* been sort of comical, the mounds of mush dripping from the astonished faces of the ladies around the table. And Mrs. Adams had wanted sugar—just not in her hair.

"If you had been there it never would have happened," Lydia said, feeling a little better with Katie's view of the disaster. "I would have had your help instead of trying to do it all myself."

She looked at Jenna. "I'm sorry if I embarrassed you and your mother. I really was trying to do my best, but when that door swung around and smacked my backside . . ."

Her voice trailed off and she shook her head. Things like the bridge-party disaster never happened to Jenna. How could Jenna understand or be sympathetic when she was born under a lucky star instead of a thunder cloud?

Then Lydia heard a chuckle.

"The door got you?" Jenna said between laughs. "I can just see it. You probably went hurtling to your face."

Jenna held her stomach as she shook with laughter. Lydia grimaced. She didn't think it was that funny.

"Did one of those globs of gunk hit my mom?" Jenna asked.

71

"Right in the face," Lydia said sheepishly.

Jenna laughed harder. "I never did like those hors d'oeuvres she makes for her bridge party," she admitted between bouts of laughter.

Lydia smiled and chuckled a little. "No one seemed very hungry after the pink and orange flying saucers attacked," she confided. "Maybe your mother will be afraid to make them again."

Jenna wiped the tears of laughter from her eyes and smiled at Lydia. "Don't worry about it," she said. "Once I poured coffee for Mrs. Whitton—right in her lap. I never knew she could move so fast."

Lydia could just picture Mrs. Whitton jumping from her chair and trying to be ladylike in the process. She chuckled again. It was nice to know Jenna goofed up once in a while too.

Suddenly Lydia remembered. Coffee hadn't gone in someone's lap. But it had stained Jenna's pinafore. She looked guiltily at Jenna.

"I spilled coffee too," she admitted. "But it wasn't on one of the ladies. It was on your dress."

Jenna hesitated a moment. "Which dress?" she asked.

"The pink one with the white pinafore," Lydia said cautiously. "At least the pinafore used to be white."

"Oh, that one," Jenna said, relief evident in her

72

voice. "Mom picked that one. I always thought it made me look too much like Alice in Wonderland."

Lydia let her breath out slowly. At least she hadn't ruined one of Jenna's favorite dresses. On the other hand, now she didn't have an excuse to give away one of Sharon's old outfits. It was too bad—she knew just the one she'd like to get rid of.

When they got to Forest Hills, Lydia and Jenna said good-bye to Katie and headed toward their lockers. Lydia was starting to feel better about the previous night's mishap.

"So what did you do last night?" she asked Jenna.

"I helped Sharon practice her cheers. She even taught me to do one," Jenna said.

With her back to Lydia, Jenna couldn't see the disappointment flash across Lydia's face. Watching Sharon practice her cheers was fun, but actually having her sister teach her a cheer was a special treat to Lydia. Sharon didn't usually have the time or the patience to coach her.

"Sharon said I was pretty good," Jenna continued, unaware of the hurt look on Lydia's face. "She said I should try out for the cheering squad in junior high."

It was all Lydia could do to fight back the tears threatening to spill over. She had bombed trying to fill Jenna's role as waitress last night. Yet Jenna fit into her life better than Lydia did. Everyone loved Jenna, even Sharon.

"You're lucky to have an older sister like Sharon," Jenna said.

Lydia whirled around to face Jenna, blinking rapidly to clear her vision. "You try doing her chores and wearing her hand-me-downs and having her treat you like a royal pain in the butt," Lydia cried. "Then we'd see how lucky you feel."

She turned and rushed down the hall, anxious to get away. Of course, as her luck would have it, she ran in the wrong direction. Mr. Henke stood in the homeroom doorway as Lydia realized her mistake.

"I didn't know you were so excited about school, Lydia," Mr. Henke said. "Rushing to class before the bell rings?"

His lips curved but the smile didn't reach his eyes. He had the same look on his face when he'd caught Chris Johnson forging a note from his mother. A shiver rippled down Lydia's spine.

"By the way, I hear you especially love social studies." At the blank expression on Lydia's face, Mr. Henke added, "I talked to your father at the bank yesterday."

Lydia felt as if she'd just gone over the top of the roller coaster. Her stomach was still hanging in midair.

She swallowed dryly and hoped her voice wouldn't fail her.

"Sure, I love school. It's a lot of fun," she said. "Except for math. Math and I don't get along."

"I noticed," Mr. Henke replied. Then he fell silent.

Lydia moved nervously from foot to foot, staring at the pocket of Mr. Henke's shirt. She could feel his eyes boring into her.

"But you're a great teacher," Lydia rambled on. "So patient and understanding with us kids."

She stole a glance at his face. For just a second she thought he was trying not to laugh, but then he looked stern again. Maybe if she could slip away . . .

"Ah, excuse me, Mr. Henke. I think I'd better use the rest room before the bell rings," Lydia said.

She started to edge away when Mr. Henke stopped her. "All right, Lydia. But I want to see you and Jenna when the lunch bell rings. We have a few things to discuss," he added sternly.

Lydia gulped and nodded her head. Her legs moved shakily down the hall. She had to find Jenna. Of course, once Lydia found her, Jenna would want to murder her. But at least then she wouldn't have to face Mr. Henke again.

Jenna was in the rest room, combing her hair, when Lydia found her. Marcia Hancock stood beside Jenna, eyeing her shiny blond hair enviously. Lydia rushed to Jenna's side.

"I have to talk to you," Lydia said. She glanced over at Marcia. "In private."

"After how you yelled at me, Lydia Barnsworth, why should I talk to you at all?" Jenna said. She glared at Lydia, then turned back to the mirror. "Besides, Marcia was telling me about Cindy Williams's new outfit."

Lydia's mouth dropped open, then she quickly shut it. She had forgotten all about being mad at Jenna. But with the trouble they were in, there wasn't time to fight.

"I'm sorry for yelling," she said, trying her best to sound apologetic. She hung her head and glanced sideways at Jenna. Hopefully her friend would forgive her—and do it quickly.

"What were you so mad about?" Jenna asked.

Lydia grabbed Jenna's arm and pulled her toward a stall. "I'll explain later. Right now we have an emergency."

Jenna followed reluctantly as Lydia pulled her inside the bathroom stall and closed the door. "He knows," Lydia whispered frantically.

Her friend scrunched her eyebrows and peered at Lydia. "He who? And what does he know?"

Lydia grabbed both of Jenna's arms and stood with her nose inches away from Jenna's face. "Mr. Henke. He wants to see us after the lunch bell," she said.

76

"So?"

"So, he talked to my dad yesterday at the bank. And he was saying how much I liked social studies," Lydia whispered so shrilly her throat ached.

Jenna's eyes widened and she held perfectly still. Lydia groaned. Jenna might be smart in math, but her brain always seemed to freeze when they were in a pinch. She shook Jenna's arms urgently.

"What are we going to do?" Lydia asked.

It took a moment for Jenna to respond. When she did, she sounded small and frightened. "Maybe he doesn't really know. Maybe he just wants us to help him with a project. You know, since we do good in class and we're best friends and all . . ."

Her voice trailed off. Lydia shook her head. Jenna was so naive. That was one thing about being in a big family. She could smell trouble coming a mile away. And this trouble was nipping at their heels.

"That's wishful thinking, Jen," she said slowly. "I'm afraid my rotten luck is rubbing off on both of us."

Then the bell sounded and they both jumped. Jenna flung open the door and stumbled out with Lydia right on her heels. Neither of them paid attention to Marcia Hancock, staring wide-eyed at them as they headed for homeroom.

CHAPTER 10

For once Lydia hated to see math class end. It meant she was that much closer to doom. She'd rather do a hundred fraction and story problems than face Mr. Henke at lunch.

As the final morning bell rang, Lydia stayed in her seat. The hour of judgment was near, and she could only hope Mr. Henke was a lenient judge.

Jenna stayed in her seat too. When the last sixth-grader had left the room, Mr. Henke closed the door. It sounded like the jaws of a trap snapping shut.

Slowly he walked over to stand in front of the two girls. Lydia held her breath and waited. She heard the clock tick. She heard Jenna's breathing. Silence held the room. Finally Mr. Henke cleared his throat.

"I had an interesting talk with your father, Lydia," he said slowly. "It seems he's very impressed with my social studies class."

Mr. Henke stared directly at Lydia. She couldn't raise

her head to look directly at him, but she could feel his eyes boring into her. She knew if she looked up, he'd see the guilt written all over her face.

"Do you have any idea why he was so impressed?" Mr. Henke asked quietly.

Lydia slowly raised her head, but Mr. Henke was staring at Jenna now. She could see Jenna's lower lip quiver. It wasn't fair. Jenna wasn't to blame.

"It's my fault, Mr. Henke," Lydia said. She glanced over at Jenna again. "Jenna just went along with me."

"And what did Jenna go along with?" Mr. Henke prompted.

Lydia blushed and swallowed hard, but she met her teacher's gaze. "Pretending we had an assignment to switch places for a week."

"That is a very interesting project," Mr. Henke said. "But why did you do it?"

Lydia thought frantically for a reason that would sound better than the truth. Could she say she thought she might be allergic to her dog and wanted to see how she felt away from him? No, she couldn't blame Jake. He was her best friend at home. It was the rest of her family she was allergic to.

Mr. Henke waited silently. Lydia wanted to scream "My brothers and sisters were driving me nuts," but then she'd be in trouble for yelling in school. She sighed and shrugged her shoulders.

"I'm the middle of five kids," she said slowly. "I just wanted to see how it felt to be the only kid in the house."

She hung her head and waited. It sounded pretty weak when she said it aloud, but at least it was the truth. And after all the lies, it felt good to say it.

Mr. Henke was silent for so long that Lydia couldn't stand the suspense. She raised her head to meet his gaze, ready to face the consequences.

"I think I understand," Mr. Henke said gently. "I grew up in a large family too. Sometimes it's not easy to be one of many.

"But," he continued, "you used my class to lie to your parents. And the best punishment I can think of is to make your project official. I'll expect a thousand-word report from each of you on my desk Monday morning."

Lydia blinked and stared openmouthed at Mr. Henke. A thousand words! That would take forever. But considering the type of punishment she had imagined . . .

"It'll be the best report I've ever written," she promised. And the last time I pull a stunt like this, she added silently to herself. It's been nothing but trouble since the first white lie.

"I do hope you really learn something," Mr. Henke said. "In fact, I might use it as a real project for next year's class."

So far, Lydia thought, she had learned that sometimes

it was nice to have an extra hand around to keep you from making a fool of yourself. But learning that wasn't worth the price of a thousand-word report, though she wasn't going to say so. After all, Mr. Henke could change his mind and put them in detention for the rest of the school year.

"I guess you girls had better get some lunch before the period is over," he said. "But remember, I expect you to complete this project you started and have your reports on my desk Monday morning."

Lydia and Jenna both nodded silently as they slipped out of their desks and headed for the door. A thousand-word report was more than Lydia wrote in her journal in a week, but at least it was better than detention or being grounded.

Suddenly another thought struck Lydia like a bolt of lightning. She stopped and whirled around to face Mr. Henke again.

"Did you tell my dad there wasn't a social-studies project?"

Mr. Henke gave her an odd look, but Lydia wasn't worried about what he thought. She could only think how surprised and disappointed her parents would be hearing the truth from her teacher.

"No, I didn't," Mr. Henke said. Before she could let out a sigh of relief he added, "I thought I should let you explain after your week is over."

Lydia's relief changed into a hard lump in the pit of her stomach. He was right. She would have to tell her parents everything. And she would probably be grounded until she turned eighteen.

Slowly Lydia joined Jenna and they walked out into the hallway. Neither of them said a word until they were halfway down the hall.

"A thousand-word report," Jenna moaned. "I'd rather do two extra pages of math."

Lydia gagged. "You've got to be kidding. Writing a report is easy compared to math problems."

"Easy for you," Jenna retorted. "You know I can't write very well."

A sting of guilt prickled Lydia's conscience. She had dragged Jenna into this scheme. Now Jenna had to write a report too. And Jenna didn't even keep a journal like she did.

"I'll help you write your report," Lydia said. "We can write them together this weekend."

Jenna merely grimaced at her as they got in the lunch line. Lydia thought about taking back her offer, but she knew Jenna wouldn't stay mad for long. Besides, it felt good to be able to help her with something after all the times Jenna had helped Lydia with math.

The sixth-grade girls' table was almost empty by the time Jenna and Lydia sat down. Only Marcia Hancock and Cindy Williams were still there. Marcia smiled at Lydia and Jenna.

"I was wondering what happened to you two. Why did you stay after class was over?" Marcia asked.

Lydia frowned. That was all she needed. If Marcia "The Mouth" Hancock found out about the trouble they were in, the whole school would know about it before long. Even Katie's second-grade class would probably hear about it before the day was over, and she doubted Katie would keep it a secret at home.

"Nothing much," Lydia said, trying to sound nonchalant. "He just wanted to talk to us about a special project."

"Of course," Marcia said with a snicker. "A special project." She smiled across the table as if she knew all their secrets. "Does this special project have anything to do with bears?"

Lydia stared at Marcia. Was she crazy? Why would they be talking to Mr. Henke about bears?

When she heard Jenna gasp, it occurred to Lydia what Marcia was thinking. Marcia's next comment confirmed it.

"I suppose Tom Bennett will have to see Mr. Henke next about a special project."

Lydia shook her head and started to laugh. Marcia thought she was so smart. But this time it would be

Marcia who got embarrassed when everyone found out her story was wrong.

Then Lydia glanced at Jenna, and her laughter died in her throat before a sound came out. Jenna's face burned as brightly as Tom's usually did. If the two of them were together, someone would be calling the fire department.

"Did you say anything to Tom?" Jenna demanded.

Her blue eyes glittered like sparks from the fire in her face. Lydia stared in fascination. She had never seen her friend so angry before. Not even the time Erik had taken the speakers out of Jenna's new boom box—and found out they weren't removable.

Marcia stammered under Jenna's furious gaze. "N-nothing much. Just that Lydia said Mr. Henke had found out."

When Jenna continued to glare at her, Marcia turned toward Lydia. "I just assumed you were talking about the other night at the carnival. So I thought someone should warn Tom," Marcia said defensively.

Jenna exploded. "You're always assuming things and jumping to conclusions. And three-fourths of the time you're wrong! Why don't you just mind your own business for a change!"

Lydia would have cheered if she hadn't been so shocked. Jenna had never told anyone off before. In fact, she rarely even stood up for herself. And the look on Marcia's face made Lydia wish she had Sharon's camera. For once The Mouth had nothing to say.

Jenna stood up to move away from the table. "I've got to go find Tom," Jenna said. "He's probably worried about being called to the principal's office after what she said."

Lydia scrambled to keep up with Jenna. She followed her out to the playground, then nearly collided with her when Jenna stopped to scan the crowd of boys playing basketball.

"Do you really think Tom took her seriously?" Lydia asked.

"Who knows if anyone takes Marcia seriously," Jenna said. "But everyone listens to her, anyway."

Just then the ball bounced off the paved court area, and there was Tom running after it. He picked up the ball, then stopped, staring in their direction. Jenna took a deep breath and walked over to where he was standing.

"Hi," Tom said. His cheeks were turning a deeper color of red under the flush he already had from playing basketball, but he didn't turn away.

"Marcia didn't know what she was talking about," Jenna blurted out. "Our talk with Mr. Henke had nothing to do with the other night."

Tom smiled slowly. "I didn't think it did. I told Marcia to shut up and mind her own business."

A smile crept across Jenna's face. "So did I."

For a minute they stood there, smiling at each other as Lydia watched. Then someone from the crowd of boys yelled for Tom to bring the ball back.

"See you later," Tom said. He sauntered back to the basketball court, glancing back once with a smile for Jenna.

Lydia shook her head in astonishment. Why couldn't everything work out for her the way it did for Jenna? Jenna had told off Marcia The Mouth, had Benny the stuffed bear to keep her company, and still had Tom smiling like a fool at her. Lydia had a thousand-word report to write, no money for her work as a waitress, and would probably be grounded the rest of her life!

It just wasn't fair, Lydia thought. Even as an only child, she was a pickle scrunched in the middle.

CHAPTER 11

Lydia walked slowly through the front door of the Taylors' house after the bus dropped her off. For once she had finished all her work in class and didn't have any homework to do. She should have been elated, but all she could think about was the paper she had to write and how upset her parents were going to be. And to top it off, her best friend had been too happy to notice that she was upset.

Mrs. Taylor was in the sunroom, off the kitchen, when Lydia went in search of a snack. She smiled as Lydia came through the door.

"There are freshly baked cookies on the counter if you want something to eat," Mrs. Taylor said. "After the mess last night, I didn't think either of us could stand to look at a paté or a mousse."

"Yeah, well, I'm really sorry about how last night turned out," Lydia said, her voice sounding small and frightened to her own ears.

"Don't worry about it," Mrs. Taylor said. "Mistakes happen. And I've left your pay for three hours' work on the counter."

Lydia's gaze flew across the countertop, stopping on a small pile of dollar bills. She couldn't believe it.

"I don't deserve any money, Mrs. Taylor," Lydia protested. "Not after the way I ruined your party."

Mrs. Taylor laughed and came into the kitchen to stand beside Lydia. "It was certainly more excitement than we usually get. But everyone threw in to tip you." She shrugged her shoulders and grinned at Lydia. "My friends who didn't have to wear the hors d'oeuvres thought the scene was hilarious and enjoyed the entertainment. The rest of us chipped in because we'd love to see you do it again—only to the other end of the table next time."

Lydia could feel the heat of her embarrassment all the way to the tips of her ears. She'd die before agreeing to serve the bridge club again. Of course, that didn't mean she couldn't take the money if Mrs. Taylor was going to insist.

"Thanks," she said as she stuffed the bills into her pocket. Her stomach rumbled, reminding Lydia why she had come into the kitchen in the first place. A cellophane-wrapped package on the counter caught her eye, and she moved over to investigate.

"Hope you like raisin-oatmeal cookies," Mrs. Taylor

said. "When I smelled them at the bakery I couldn't resist."

It wasn't her favorite, but Lydia thought she could manage to eat a few.

"Do you have more math to do tonight?" Mrs. Taylor asked.

"No," Lydia answered between bites of cookie. "I got everything done in class."

"That's great," Mrs. Taylor said. "I have to run over to Claudia Adams's house, and with Jenna's father working late this evening, I felt bad about leaving you alone. But if you don't have homework, you could come along."

Lydia thought about Mrs. Adams's son Tony. If she went with Mrs. Taylor, Tony would ask questions she wouldn't want to answer. And as tired as she was of covering up the truth, she wasn't ready for their secret to be exposed again either.

"Thanks, but if you don't mind, I'll just stay here and watch television," Lydia said. "I don't get my choice of programs very often."

Mrs. Taylor smiled sympathetically and nodded her head. Lydia hurried from the room, her stomach churning into knots. She didn't deserve any sympathy, but she couldn't say that to Mrs. Taylor. All she wanted was to hide in her room.

Her own room in her own house, Lydia realized suddenly. She wanted to curl up on her bed, write in her journal, and listen to the chaotic noises that always rumbled through the house. But that was crazy. She had a room to herself here, not one shared with a pesky little sister. And she was determined to enjoy it for the few days she had left.

After supper, Lydia watched Mrs. Taylor drive away. She had the entire house to herself. Surely there was something fun to do.

She flopped down on the sofa in the family room and grabbed the television remote control. It was wonderful to be able to flick through the channels herself. At home there was always a battle over the remote, and half the time one of her parents simply took it away. It wasn't nearly as much fun to channel-surf when you had to walk over to the television set and turn the knob.

After flipping through every station several times, Lydia gave up and turned off the TV. Nothing looked interesting.

Aimlessly she walked around the room, then out into the kitchen. The phone was in her hand, the number dialed, before she really thought about what she was doing. By then it didn't seem to matter.

"H'lo. Who is this?"

Lydia recognized Erik's voice and was tempted to hang up and try later. Her little brother could be just as troublesome answering the phone as he was at the door. Instead she used her most sophisticated voice and tried to bluff her way past him.

"May I please speak to Jenna Taylor."

A moment of silence came across the phone connection. Lydia put her hand over her mouth so she wouldn't laugh. She could imagine the puzzled look on Erik's face as he tried to figure out who was calling.

"She's outside," he said. Then he was silent again.

"Please get her," Lydia said. She tried to make herself sound like Mrs. Taylor so Erik would get Jenna right away.

"Can't."

She could scarcely believe her ears. What was Erik up to? "Pardon me?"

"She's doing a cheer with Sharon. Then she's gotta listen to a new joke I learnt. She don't have time for you today, Lydia."

She gasped. How did he know it was her? Before she could utter a word, the phone connection began buzzing in her ear. Erik had hung up on her!

Lydia put down the receiver and stared into space. What a monster. How had he known it was her? And how dare he hang up when she wasn't finished talking!

But what was there to say, she asked herself. If Jenna and Sharon were practicing cheers, Jenna wouldn't want to stop just to talk to her. Tears burned at the edges of

91

her eyelids. Erik had been partially right. No one had time for her today.

Lydia rubbed her eyes and sniffed, silently assuring herself that she didn't care in the least. She'd microwave some popcorn, find something on the TV, and have a party—all by herself.

She settled into the sofa cushions, a bowl of popcorn nestled in her lap. An old horror movie, *The Mummy's Curse,* was on the Movie Channel. If she were at home, her parents wouldn't let her watch it because Erik and Katie could have nightmares. That didn't matter to Lydia. She couldn't be frightened by an old black-and-white movie.

An hour later, during a commercial break, Lydia sat upright on the couch. She had heard something. She was sure of it. Something more than the creaks and groans of the house.

Carefully she sat up, shifting the empty bowl from her lap to the table, and listened intently. Footsteps. There were definitely footsteps coming from another part of the house. Lydia's eyes widened. With the family room at the back of the house, a burglar must have thought the house was empty. Now he was inside and coming toward her.

Lydia scrambled to her feet and looked frantically around the room. She needed a weapon to defend herself with. But the remote control was too small to make an impact—and the pillows too soft to hurt. The lack of obvious choices forced her to hurry into the next room. Surely the laundry room would have a decent weapon.

She grabbed a broom from the closet, tested its balance in her hand, and decided it was as good as she would find. Then she silently positioned herself at the laundry-room doorway, the broom arched behind her and ready to swing.

Silence settled over the house again. Lydia strained against the darkness, hoping to hear a sound yet wishing she were wrong about the intruder. Then she heard it again. Footsteps headed in her direction.

She held her breath and closed her eyes, but only for a moment. The footsteps were getting closer by the second. She tensed. Then as a shadow moved forward across the door, Lydia swung her broom.

"Owww," the intruder yelled. The voice sounded vaguely familiar to Lydia.

"Mr. Taylor?" Lydia leaned forward from her hiding place and looked at the figure holding the side of his head. "Oh, Mr. Taylor. I'm so sorry."

She tried to help him up, but Mr. Taylor merely held his hands palm outward as if warding off an evil spirit.

"Don't worry. I'm all right," he muttered. He shook his head slightly as if trying to clear the fog from his brain. After a few moments he looked directly at her, and a small smile lightened his features. "Jean told me

93

to watch out, that you were a force to be reckoned with. I just didn't realize she meant physically.''

She could only stare as he shook his head again and muttered under his breath. Whatever he was saying, she didn't think she'd be asked to stay another week.

When Katie and Jenna got on the bus the next morning, they were talking excitedly about the plans for Jenna's last evening at the Barnsworths' house.

"Mike's going to pick out a movie rental and Mom said she'd make popcorn," Katie said. Her curls bounced as she spoke. "Erik wants to do some jokes for intermission, and even Sharon is going to be home. It'll be a regular party."

Lydia tried to smile, but her throat felt tight and ached. "That's nice," she muttered.

"What are you going to do?" Katie asked.

Lydia bit her lip and thought about making up some outrageous party plans. But Jenna would probably guess she wasn't telling the truth.

She shrugged her shoulders. "I don't know. I guess it'll be a surprise."

Jenna gave her a curious glance, but didn't say anything. Lydia wondered whether the Taylors went out every Thursday evening and Jenna didn't want to tell her. That would be her luck—to sit at the Taylors' house alone while a party was going on at her old house.

She sighed and wished there were someone else to blame for her awful week. Maybe she could blame Jenna for making her believe being an only child was so much fun. Or she could blame Erik and Katie for driving her to it. The problem was, in her heart Lydia knew there was no one else to blame but herself.

The day's classes were a relief to Lydia. They gave her something to do besides feel sorry for herself. Of course, Mr. Henke piling on the math work wasn't exactly what she had in mind, but it did keep her occupied.

When the lunch bell rang, Lydia didn't want to sit at the sixth-grade table. If Jenna said one word about the party that night or if Marcia Hancock bugged her to know about Mr. Henke's project, she'd probably cry. Then she'd be even more miserable.

"Wow, did you get all that math work done?" Jenna asked as they sat down. "I've still got ten problems to do."

Lydia looked up in surprise. She had concentrated so hard on her math, so she wouldn't think about the mess she was in, that she had gotten it all done. And for once Jenna hadn't finished.

"It was a lot," she agreed. "But I got them done."

When Jenna stared wide-eyed at her, Lydia added with a half smile, "Of course, they're probably all wrong."

"I doubt it," Jenna said. "You're actually pretty good at math, even if you do hate it."

Lydia shrugged and bit into her slice of pizza. She'd hate to have to be this miserable just to do well in math.

"Have you guys heard the latest?" Marcia asked as she set her tray down on the table across from Jenna and Lydia. She didn't wait for anyone to answer. "Brian Temple passed Cindy Williams a note in English class. And Mrs. Bowlby took it."

Marcia's eyes glittered with excitement. "It was probably a love note. They both had to stay after class."

Lydia glanced over at Jenna and rolled her eyes toward the ceiling. At least Marcia wasn't talking about them anymore. Now it was Cindy's turn to suffer The Mouth.

Jenna pursed her lips and frowned across the table at Marcia. "How do you know what it said?" Jenna demanded. "For all you know it could have been a blank piece of paper. And even if it was a love note, it's really none of your business, Marcia."

Jenna picked up her tray and headed for the cafeteria exit. Lydia watched her leave, then glanced over at the shocked expression on Marcia's face. Maybe this week as a middle child had been good for Jenna. At least she was no longer shy about speaking her mind.

Lydia popped the last bite of pizza into her mouth

and picked up her tray. It had definitely been an interesting week.

Interesting wasn't quite the word that came to Lydia's mind later that evening. She sat across from Mrs. Taylor, playing a word game. She should have been happy that both the Taylors were home with her, just like a family. But somehow the quiet evening wasn't what she had expected.

"It's your turn," Mrs. Taylor said. "You're still beating me by ten points."

Lydia stared at the words on the board. Normally she loved playing games. Of course, that was when she was trying to beat Mike or Sharon or Katie. It wasn't as much fun beating Jenna's mother.

As the pieces disappeared and the board slowly filled with words, Mrs. Taylor leaned back in her chair. "I think you're too good for me, Lydia," she said. "How about if we declare you the winner and go out for ice cream?"

"Great idea," Lydia said with more enthusiasm than she'd shown all evening.

Mrs. Taylor laughed. "I thought you might like that. Come on. Let's see if Ben wants a break from his paperwork to join us."

Later, as Lydia settled into the booth with Mr. and Mrs. Taylor and her hot-fudge sundae, she told herself that being an only child was okay, but being a middle kid wasn't too bad either. They each had their ups and downs. And being the only child for an ice-cream treat was definitely a positive.

CHAPTER 12

Lydia was out of bed early. She had her bag packed by the time Mrs. Taylor announced that breakfast was ready.

"I'll be right there," Lydia answered.

She turned back to the room and grimaced. Jenna would have a cow if she saw her room in such a mess. Lydia struggled with the covers on the bed, smoothing them as best she could. Then she quickly straightened Jenna's record collection and knickknacks. The room looked almost as perfect as Jenna kept it. Grabbing her schoolbag, she went down to her last breakfast with the Taylors.

"Good morning, Lydia," Mr. Taylor said, lowering the newspaper to smile at her. "Are you anxious to go home today?"

Lydia smiled hesitantly. She didn't want to hurt the Taylors' feelings, but she was ready to go home. Of course, with the way she had messed up the week, the Taylors were probably just as anxious to see her go.

"Well, it'll be nice to sleep in my own bed," she said. "Jenna's bed is a little harder than I'm used to."

Mr. Taylor chuckled. "I know what you mean. It's the bed and the different night noises that keep you awake." He winked at Lydia. "Guess you won't need your broom once you're back in your own house."

Even though she knew he was teasing, Lydia couldn't stop the hot flush racing to her cheeks. She tried to smile, but her face wasn't cooperating.

Mrs. Taylor set a plate of French toast in front of Lydia. "Don't tease her about that, Ben," Mrs. Taylor said. "I'm sure Lydia would like to forget it."

She turned toward Lydia and smiled. "We really have enjoyed having you here. And I'll bet your family will be happy to have you back."

Lydia stopped a moment and thought about what Mrs. Taylor had said. Jenna had fit perfectly into Lydia's family. Jenna had fixed Katie's hair, laughed at Erik's jokes, gotten Mike to help with her math, and even had Sharon teach her cheers. Why would they want her back? They'd probably rather keep Jenna.

A heavy weight lodged in the pit of Lydia's stomach. She was ready to go home, but was her family ready to take her back?

French toast was one of Lydia's favorite breakfasts, but she found it hard to swallow past the lump in her throat. One slice was all she could manage to eat.

"I'm not very hungry this morning," she said apologetically to Mrs. Taylor. "I think I'll go and wait for the bus."

"You're sure you don't want another slice?" Mrs. Taylor asked.

Lydia shook her head. "See you this afternoon," she said.

Mrs. Taylor gave her a hug as she went out to meet the bus, and Lydia smiled to herself. Even if nothing else had gone right with her week, at least it was nice to have two mothers to count on.

Lydia's excited mood was beginning to return when the bus stopped at the Barnsworths' house. Katie and Jenna sat down next to her.

"Are you ready to have your own room back?" Lydia asked Jenna.

Jenna glanced over at Katie, then shrugged her shoulders. "There are a few albums I miss hearing," Jenna said slowly. "And it's definitely quieter at my house."

Lydia grinned at how tactful Jenna was trying to be. Katie had probably talked in her sleep and kept Jenna awake all night. She could almost see dark circles under her friend's blue eyes.

"I'll get off the bus with you after school so we can get your bag. Then we can walk over to your house to get my stuff," Lydia said.

Katie looked up at Jenna. Her eyes were stretched

wide, making her curls look even wilder than usual. "I'll miss you, Jenna," Katie said sadly.

"I'm not leaving Blooming Prairie," Jenna said with a laugh. "I'll still see you."

The corners of Katie's mouth turned down and her lower lip pushed forward. "Yeah, but it won't be the same," Katie said.

The lump in Lydia's stomach grew heavier, as if one slice of French toast had added ten pounds. Then when Katie reached over to hold Jenna's hand, the lump in her stomach became a huge bowling ball. Lydia turned to look out the bus window and wished she could pretend the last week had never happened.

The day flew by for Lydia. Social studies was the last class of the day. Usually on Fridays, she watched the clock tick off the minutes until the bell rang, but today she dreaded the end of class.

When the bell rang, Lydia stacked her books and followed the crowd toward the door. She hoped to slip quickly past Mr. Henke before he said anything. She'd been avoiding talking directly to him since she and Jenna had gotten their "special assignment."

"Lydia," Mr. Henke said.

Her heart sank into the pit of her stomach. She stopped and looked timidly back at her teacher.

"Don't forget your assignment is due Monday," he said.

Lydia suppressed a groan and nodded her head. How could she forget, she moaned silently to herself. The entire disastrous week loomed constantly over her head.

Jenna was waiting at the locker for her. "What did Mr. Henke want?" Jenna asked. "I heard him say your name after I got out the door."

Lydia wrinkled her nose. "He just wanted to make sure I remembered our assignment for Monday. I'd like to forget it and this whole week," Lydia muttered.

"Well, it was your idea," Jenna reminded her. "Besides, it wasn't so bad."

Easy for you to say, Lydia wanted to tell Jenna. But she didn't want to have to explain what she meant. And she certainly didn't want to admit that she was anxious to go home.

"Let's get going," Lydia said grumpily. "I don't want to miss the bus."

Jenna looked curiously at her, but Lydia ignored it. Being nervous always made her grouchy. And she was definitely feeling nervous.

By the time the bus reached the Barnsworths' house, Lydia could have sworn ants were running up and down under her skin. It didn't make sense. After all, she was just coming home.

Katie raced off the bus and around to the back door

as Lydia and Jenna walked down the driveway. "I'll tell Mom we're home," Katie called back to them. "She'll want to say good-bye to Jenna."

Lydia rolled her eyes as Jenna looked at her with a smile. She tried to smile back, but it was hard when her mind kept yelling "What about me!"

"Hi, girls," Mrs. Barnsworth said as she came into the kitchen. "Would you like a snack before you go over to Jenna's house? I made chocolate-chip cookies this afternoon."

Lydia inhaled deeply and let her breath out in a sigh. This was how houses should smell, warm and gooey. She liked it much better than pine aerosol.

"Thanks, but I'd better hurry home," Jenna said. "My mom is probably waiting for me."

Mrs. Barnsworth gave Jenna's shoulders a squeeze. "I'm sure she is. And we're going to miss you too."

Lydia looked away. Her mother had hugged Jenna before, but today it felt funny to watch. Sort of like Jenna was really the daughter here and she was a visitor.

"Let's grab your bag and get going," Lydia said. "We wouldn't want to keep your mom waiting."

Jenna led the way upstairs. Lydia trailed along behind her, looking around at the pictures on the wall. Everything looked the same, but somehow it felt different. It was like she didn't even know the way to her own room.

Katie was sitting at the desk in the bedroom. She

looked up as Jenna and Lydia came through the door-way, folding her arms across the paper in front of her. Jenna walked over to Katie and ruffled her curls affectionately.

"Remember to brush your hair every night like I showed you, squirt," Jenna said. "It'll make your curls shine."

Katie smiled up at Jenna, and an invisible hand punched Lydia in the stomach. Squirt was *her* nickname for Katie. Now Jenna was using it—and Katie wasn't objecting.

"I made something for you," Katie said shyly. She held out the piece of paper to Jenna.

"Thanks," Jenna said. She leaned over and hugged Katie. "I'll put it on my bulletin board."

Lydia stood on tiptoe to peer over Jenna's shoulder. The paper had a picture of two girls, the larger one fixing the smaller girl's hair. The names Jenna and Katie were scrawled across the top.

"We'd better go," Lydia said abruptly. She grabbed Jenna's bag and turned toward the door. She didn't care if Jenna followed or not. She had to get out of there.

By the time she got to the living room, Jenna had caught up with her. "Slow down, Lydia," Jenna complained. "We're not in that big a hurry."

Erik appeared before Lydia could get Jenna out the front door.

"Jenna, wait!" Erik yelled. "You have to see what I can do."

Erik held up his hands to display two pieces of a spaceship. He pushed the pieces together, wiggling and prodding them into each other. Then triumphantly he held the spaceship aloft.

"See, I can do it. Just like you showed me."

"That's great," Jenna said. "I knew you could do it. Bet someday you'll be a famous engineer."

The grin Erik gave Jenna was all sunshine and happiness. He threw his arms around her legs and gave them a squeeze.

"Thanks, Jen," Erik said. "I'm glad you came and stayed with us."

Then Erik turned and ran out of the room. Jenna stood staring at the doorway, a soft smile on her lips. Lydia blinked rapidly. Maybe it was too late to get Jenna out of the house.

CHAPTER 13

Lydia returned home with her bag and crept quietly up the stairs. Her heart raced as if she were a burglar sneaking into someone's house. She knew it was silly, but her body wasn't listening to her.

She opened the door to the bedroom, half expecting to find Katie snooping in her things. But Katie was still sitting at the desk, working diligently at something.

"What are you doing?" Lydia asked curiously.

Katie hunched farther over her work but didn't look up. "Just a special project I have to do," Katie answered.

Lydia knew all about special projects. They could be a real pain.

"Do you need some help?" Lydia asked.

"No," Katie said quickly. "Jenna helped me get started on it last night."

Jenna. Lydia was getting tired of hearing her family mention Jenna. If they liked Jenna so much, maybe she should trade places again—permanently.

Lydia stomped out the door and went downstairs to the family room. Erik was sitting on the floor, surrounded by pieces of plastic. They looked like they had once been his favorite helicopter.

"Need some help?" Lydia asked, hiding her smile as Erik scratched his head, a look of serious concentration on his face.

"No. I can do it," Erik muttered. "I watched real careful when I took it apart. Jenna said I'd be a famous engineer one day."

Lydia frowned. She doubted Erik would make it as an engineer in the next half hour. Maybe in twenty or thirty years. What was Jenna thinking, encouraging Erik to take his toys apart? In no time at all he wouldn't have a single toy to play with.

She wandered into the kitchen for a cookie. At least her mother's baking hadn't changed in a week. The cookies were just the way she liked them—munchy around the edges and gooey in the middle.

"Can I help with supper?" Lydia asked as her mother appeared in the kitchen doorway.

"Thanks, but you just relax and enjoy your first evening home," Mrs. Barnsworth said. "Sharon promised to be home in time to help."

Lydia tried not to gape with her mouth wide open, but she could hardly believe her ears. Sharon never volunteered to help with supper if she thought Lydia would

108

be around to do it. Either Sharon was sick or it had something to do with Jenna's stay. She strongly suspected it was Jenna. But if it got her out of work, why should she care?

She walked outside and plopped down on the back steps, staring out into the yard. The trouble was, she did care. No one seemed to need her help or want her around. She might as well have stayed at the Taylors' house for all her family noticed.

Lydia propped her elbows on her knees and leaned her head on her palms. How had she gotten into this mess?

Just then Mike came strolling around the side of the house. Lydia sat up straight and watched him come toward her.

"Hi, Mike," she said. "Want to play catch before supper? You could practice your pitching."

Lydia reached forward and picked up an old tennis ball from the grass. It was Jake's ball, but it would do for playing catch. At least it wasn't all slobbery at the moment.

"Naw," Mike said as he climbed the stairs behind her. "I've got things to do. Maybe Jake will play fetch."

Lydia waited until the door slammed shut, then she slouched forward on her knees again. No one wanted her around. Everything had changed—all because of Jenna.

She rolled the ball in her hands. Jake liked to play fetch. At least her dog wouldn't have turned against her.

She stood up and whistled loudly. Then she whistled again. From behind the garage she heard an answering bark.

"Here, Jake," she called. The golden retriever bounded out into the yard and headed straight for her. He almost knocked her over when he reached her.

"Good boy," Lydia said. "At least you're still my buddy."

She hugged Jake and scratched him behind the ears. It was his favorite place to be scratched. Jake wagged his tail and gave her a wet kiss.

"Yeah, I love you too, boy," Lydia whispered, burying her face in the soft fur around Jake's neck. It felt good to know someone was happy to see her, even if he was just a dog.

Lydia showed Jake the ball hidden in her hand. "Fetch? Jake want to play fetch?"

She threw the ball across the yard and watched the dog race after it. Just as Jake reached the tennis ball and picked it up, Lydia heard a kid's voice from a neighboring yard. Jake froze, his ears pricked forward. Then he dropped the ball and bounded off in the direction of the voice.

"Jake!" Lydia yelled. "Bring me the ball. Come on, boy." But the furry beast didn't reappear.

"Stupid dog," Lydia muttered. "Go ahead and desert me like everyone else. See if I care."

She sank down on the ground and plucked a handful of grass, throwing it into the air. Why was her family being so mean? Even her dog didn't have time for her. What could Jenna have done to a dog?

Suddenly Lydia sighed. She couldn't blame Jenna. After all, she was the one who had started this escapade. Jenna had just gone along with her. She'd thought it would be wonderful to be an only child, but it hadn't turned out that way. Being an only child had been kind of boring and lonely, especially since she was used to so much commotion going on.

Lydia sighed again. Being the pickle in the middle wasn't always fun, but at least it wasn't boring. And she never had to worry about being lonely.

Whether or not she'd always liked it, she'd known the spot between Mike and Katie was hers in the family lineup. And at the moment she'd give anything to feel smooshed in the middle again. Then at least she'd know her family had missed her as much as she had missed them.

The back door opened and Katie stuck her head out. "Mom says it's time for supper."

Lydia got up and brushed the grass off her clothes. Maybe if she was super nice, her family would accept her back. Of course, once she confessed the truth about her week at Jenna's, they might never talk to her again.

She trudged slowly into the house and washed her hands at the sink. Everyone must have sat down to eat since no one was in the kitchen. They hadn't even waited for her, Lydia thought unhappily. She'd probably have to eat the leftovers, like Jake sometimes did.

Lydia walked into the dining room and froze in her tracks.

"Welcome home!" her family yelled.

Katie and Erik were holding a banner with the words WELCOME HOME LYDIA scrawled across it in crayon. The last sheet of paper attached to the banner had a picture of seven people. Lydia recognized Katie's handiwork, especially Katie's portrait of herself with beautiful curls. She didn't know what to say.

"We're glad to have you back," Lydia's mother said. "And I made all your favorites for supper."

Lydia gazed dazedly around the table. There was spaghetti and meatballs, cheesy garlic bread, and red Jell-O. It looked wonderful.

"Mom made us do the banner," Katie said with a grin. Her eyes twinkled mischievously as she put down the banner and took her seat next to Lydia.

"Katie," Mrs. Barnsworth said, a warning note in her voice.

Lydia didn't mind. Her whole family was smiling at

her as they took their seats around the dinner table, even Sharon and Mike. Maybe, just maybe, they really had missed her.

The usual noise and commotion that went with a meal at the Barnsworth house filled the dining room. Lydia listened happily as she ate her spaghetti. Before the meal was over, Erik reached for a piece of bread and knocked over his milk. Lydia watched the white river splash across the table. It hit the plate of cheesy garlic bread, ran along the crack of the table leaf, and dripped off the edge of the table—right into Lydia's lap.

Yes, she thought happily to herself, she was definitely home.

Lydia pedaled leisurely on her ten-speed bike. The sun was shining, her bike was working great since Mike and her dad had fixed it, and she was on her way to Jenna's house. All was right with the world—especially since her parents hadn't grounded her.

She had thought it would be hard to confess the truth to her parents. In fact, she had gone to bed without telling them, only to lie awake worrying about it. Finally, when she couldn't stand the nagging voice in her head any longer, Lydia had slipped out to the living room, where her parents were watching the late-night news.

Lydia smiled to herself as she remembered how she'd

hung her head and stuttered for a place to begin. But once the words had started, she couldn't hold them back. She had told her parents everything. And amazingly enough, they had understood.

When she had told them about Mr. Henke finding out and turning their hoax into a real project, her father had laughed out loud.

"I figured something was going on by the look on his face," Mr. Barnsworth had said. "He didn't know what to say."

The thought of Mr. Henke at a loss for words had made Lydia giggle nervously. He wasn't such a bad teacher. After all, somebody had to teach math.

"Although you were wrong to lie to us," her mother had said, "I think writing a thousand-word report is punishment enough. It's a fair consequence for your actions."

Lydia had held her breath, waiting for a second punishment to come from her parents, but nothing had come. And when her mother had started to warn her of what would happen next time she told a lie, Lydia had rushed to reassure them she'd learned her lesson. Covering up a story was more headache than it was worth.

She pedaled faster as Jenna's house came into view. Maybe if they hurried with their reports, they could ride over to the park. It was a great day for hanging around outside.

Jenna opened the door before Lydia could ring the doorbell. "Let's get started," Jenna said. "I can't leave the house until my report is done."

Lydia gave Jenna a sympathetic look. "You told your parents?" she asked.

"Yeah, they weren't too mad," Jenna answered. "I just got lectured on telling the truth."

"Me too," Lydia said. "I guess we're pretty lucky."

Jenna nodded and led the way to her bedroom. Notepads and pens were strewn across the bed. There was even a pair of pajamas on the floor, along with several record albums.

"I see Katie taught you something in exchange for you fixing her hair," Lydia said, hiding the smile tugging at the edges of her lips.

Jenna looked quizzically at her. "What?"

"The Barnsworth method of housekeeping," she said with a laugh.

Jenna blushed, then joined in the laughter. "It's the latest bedroom design—the lived-in look," Jenna said.

The girls sat on the bed, notepads and pens in hands, and stared at the blank pages in front of them. After a minute, Jenna sighed.

"I don't know how to begin," she complained. "I'm not even sure what we're writing about."

Lydia shook her head. Jenna might be a whiz at math, but she didn't know much about writing a good story.

And with all the crazy things that happen at the Barnsworths' house, Jenna should be the one with the most to tell.

"We're supposed to write about the differences in our families," Lydia said patiently. "Like how meals are formal at your house, except for breakfast when your dad reads his newspaper and your mom is still in her robe and slippers."

"Supper is a zoo at your house, with everyone talking and passing food around the table," Jenna said thoughtfully. "And breakfast is self-serve cold cereal, with everyone eating in shifts when they get up."

"Your house is always clean and neat," Lydia said with a smile. "Except maybe your room."

"And yours has the original lived-in look," Jenna finished for her.

The two friends smiled at each other. "I could tell about being the hostess for the bridge club," Lydia suggested.

"And how the door attacked you," Jenna added with a laugh. "And I could write about having an older brother or sister to help with your homework and chores."

"Maybe I'll write how nice it is to be the center of attention sometimes, and to be able to pick all the television shows *you* want to watch," Lydia said. "But it can also be spooky being all by yourself."

"Yeah," Jenna agreed. "It's nice to have someone to talk to—but not when you're trying to sleep."

Lydia flopped back on Jenna's pillow and laughed. "I knew Katie would talk in her sleep and drive you crazy."

"Well, it did scare me the first time I heard her," Jenna admitted. She looked over at Lydia and grinned. "Don't you wish you could understand what she's saying?"

Both girls laughed, thinking about the crazy gibberish Katie mumbled in her sleep. "Believe me, she doesn't make any sense," Lydia said. "And I've tried to figure it out often enough."

Lydia sat up and set her notepad in her lap. There were so many things she wanted to write about, good points about her solitary week as well as about her real-family life. And the most important point she wanted to share was that the number of people in your family didn't really matter, as long as you had a place where you belonged.

She smiled to herself as her pen began to move along the page. Being the pickle stuck in the middle was right where she wanted to be.

Read All the Stories by
Beverly Cleary

☐ **HENRY HUGGINS**
70912-0 ($4.50 US/ $5.99 Can)

☐ **HENRY AND BEEZUS**
70914-7 ($4.50 US/ $5.99 Can)

☐ **HENRY AND THE CLUBHOUSE**
70915-5 ($4.50 US/ $6.50 Can)

☐ **ELLEN TEBBITS**
70913-9 ($4.50 US/ $5.99 Can)

☐ **HENRY AND RIBSY**
70917-1 ($4.50 US/ $5.99 Can)

☐ **BEEZUS AND RAMONA**
70918-X ($4.50 US/ $6.50 Can)

☐ **RAMONA AND HER FATHER**
70916-3 ($4.50 US/ $6.50 Can)

☐ **MITCH AND AMY**
70925-2 ($4.50 US/ $5.99 Can)

☐ **RUNAWAY RALPH**
70953-8 ($4.50 US/ $5.99 Can)

☐ **RAMONA QUIMBY, AGE 8**
70956-2 ($4.50 US/ $5.99 Can)

☐ **RIBSY**
70955-4 ($4.50 US/ $5.99 Can)

☐ **STRIDER**
71236-9 ($4.50 US/ $5.99 Can)

☐ **HENRY AND THE PAPER ROUTE**
70921-X ($4.50 US/ $6.50 Can)

☐ **RAMONA AND HER MOTHER**
70952-X ($4.50 US/ $5.99 Can)

☐ **OTIS SPOFFORD**
70919-8 ($4.50 US/ $5.99 Can)

☐ **THE MOUSE AND THE MOTORCYCLE**
70924-4 ($4.50 US/ $5.99 Can)

☐ **SOCKS**
70926-0 ($4.50 US/ $5.99 Can)

☐ **EMILY'S RUNAWAY IMAGINATION**
70923-6 ($4.50 US/ $5.99 Can)

☐ **MUGGIE MAGGIE**
71087-0 ($4.50 US/ $5.99 Can)

☐ **RAMONA THE PEST**
70954-6 ($4.50 US/ $5.99 Can)

☐ **RALPH S. MOUSE**
70957-0 ($4.50 US/ $5.99 Can)

☐ **DEAR MR. HENSHAW**
70958-9 ($4.50 US/ $5.99 Can)

☐ **RAMONA THE BRAVE**
70959-7 ($4.50 US/ $5.99 Can)

☐ **RAMONA FOREVER**
70960-6 ($4.50 US/ $5.99 Can)